'A sharply drawn world of wonder in e... fresh, innovative novel that is an ode to families, coming of age and sisterhood.' **ROGER ROBINSON**

'A truly enriching read, *Somebody Loves You* is a glorious debut novel. I took this book with me everywhere and kept returning to it. I loved every perfect choice of word and turn of phrase in this vivid and tender, poetic and beautiful book.' **SALENA GODDEN**

'Mona Arshi writes with curiosity, gentleness, and a keen eye for how even the smallest details of daily life can carry meaning. In form and content, this is a gleaming, quiet novel cut through with remarkable confidence. Reading *Somebody Loves You* was like being rocked gently – and then shaken entirely awake.' **JESSICA J LEE**

'Mona Arshi's *Somebody Loves You* opens with a gesture: a bowl filled with peat and one blue egg. The egg, swallowed, becomes one bird and then another, until "the room", as Arshi writes, "is filled with their iridescent turquoise feathers and clamour of yellow-black beaks". And this is what it was like to read this intense collection of prose works: successive gifts that activate transformations of the deepest order. A clove, a parable, a pear, a silver box, a pistol, a kitten, guidance from unexpected sources, and "incredible fables" coalesce in the way that family stories, or bed-time stories, often do: changing time in the body of the person reading or listening to them. Arshi has written a book without partitions, or boundaries. Something flows through it at the deepest level: experiences of love, care, memory and intimacy. Written with the poetic capacity to articulate the unsaid and the unknown, *Somebody Loves You* is an extraordinary novel of the day, the night, the garden, and life.' **BHANU KAPIL**

SOMEBODY

LOVES

YOU

MONA

ARSHI

SHEFFIELD – LONDON – NEW YORK

First published in 2021 by And Other Stories
Sheffield – London – New York
www.andotherstories.org

1 3 5 7 9 8 6 4 2

ISBN: 9781913505165
eBook ISBN: 9781913505172

Editor: Tara Tobler; Copy-editor: Bella Bosworth; Proofreader: Sarah Terry;
Text designed and set in Albertan Pro and Syntax by Tetragon, London;
Cover Design: Holly Ovenden; Printed and bound on acid-free,
age-resistant Munken Premium by CPI Limited, Croydon, UK.

And Other Stories gratefully acknowledge that our work is
supported using public funding by Arts Council England.

For my mother

I look for myself and am not to be found. I am of all chrysanthemum hours, bright above tall vases. I have to make of my soul an ornamental thing.

—FERNANDO PESSOA,
The Book of Disquiet

EGGS

A man is offering her a bowl. She peers inside and there is an egg nestled in light peat close to the surface. It is a small blue egg – perfect and complete. She gently lifts it out of the bowl and places it in her mouth and the egg, still warm, breaks onto her tongue, makes her retch a little but still she swallows it. She closes then reopens her eyes and a blue bird escapes from her mouth. Then another and another, until the room is filled with their iridescent turquoise feathers and clamour of yellow-black beaks.

A few settle on her head, others perch on her shoulders, but then after a few minutes and for no discernible reason they quickly flit back inside – a hymn of bodies returning as they enter back through her parted lips. Several fly into and penetrate her torso. When the last bird has gone, she closes her mouth and leaves the room.

FOXES

The day my sister tried to drag the baby fox into our house was the same day my mother had her first mental breakdown.

In many ways it was the perfect morning for a breakdown. The rain was spitting softly, the Parkers' dog just wouldn't stop barking, it went on emitting that terrible noise like it was a machine loaded with everlasting batteries. In the living room I had just finished watching a long documentary about wild kangaroos.

Upstairs there was a doctor, the Aunties, and my father of course. There was a toy: a miniature replica camera that my sister was jealous of, and she kept prising the camera from my fingers and pointing it at things she liked the look of and saying, 'See I can click! I can click!' till eventually I had to steal it away from her and hang the long leather strap around my neck. For days we had known about the foxes. They had come closer and closer to the house and had been chewing at the garden boots my mum had stored under the corrugated plastic shelter.

I went into the kitchen and the side door was open, and there was Rania crouching on the steps carrying a bundle, a blanket covering the body so that only its ears and eyes were visible.

I heard the front door click open then slam shut, the fox yelped and slipped away, and we didn't see my mother again for three whole months.

MARROW

Since infancy my sister has been stimulated by gore, guts and blood. My parents said that when she was still in her buggy, she would sniff the air, aroused by the smell of the butcher's, then unbuckle her harness and head to the spectacle of the shop window. She would be at the front of the circle, pushing forward, wanting but also *needing* to see.

For some time, my sister's most frequent questions were, 'Could you see the bone?' and, 'How much blood?'

Rania befriended Martin Higgins at school who was prone to long nosebleeds. She was always coming to his aid when he was bleeding across the school field during sports lessons, or after too much sunshine, which disturbed the delicate blood vessels in this pale and nervous boy's nostrils. Whilst the teacher struggled to stem the flow with cigar-shaped cotton rolls Rania would be by her side, holding napkins and asking, 'How many pints do you think he's leaked? When will he start clotting? Will he pass out? How long will he keep bleeding for?' (Usually about an hour and a half.) For some time, my parents harboured a belief that their eldest daughter might train as a doctor or a surgeon. It was a short-lived fantasy, as it quickly became apparent Rania wasn't the slightest bit interested in healing anything, she was just morbidly inquisitive. My parents checked their ambitions and down-graded their hopes to dentistry, followed by pharmacology, then podiatry, until, a little while later, they abandoned all hope of the sciences.

BEGINNINGS

My name is Ruby. I am skinny and superfluously tall. I am skinny because I have inherited both my parents' propensity for growing thin bones. If you met him probably you would think my father is short — he tells us he is not unusually so for an Indian man, but by European standards he is willing to concede. When my family says that I am too tall I assume they mean both in the western and Indian sense. I suppose I should say at this stage that both my parents are normalish talkers — let's get that out of the way straight off. I'm not much of a talker by whatever standards you choose to apply.

The first time I spoke out loud at school I said the word *sister* and tripped all over it. I tried a second time, and my tongue got caught on the middle-syllable hiss and hovered there. The third time? A teacher asked me a question, and I opened my mouth as a sort of formality but closed it softly, knowing with perfect certainty that nothing would ever come out again. I was certain about this the next morning and even more certain about it the day following that. I uttered absolutely nothing. It became the most certain thing in my life.

I was tested for aural dysfunction, mumps and general stupidity. For a few months I was even sent up to a clinic to sit in a room with a young doctor. She passed me a cup of broken crayons and some coloured paper to draw whatever my mind rested on. I think I knew at an early age that this doctor's job was to gently fish inside my head, to get right to the bottom of my talking problems. Because I was a pleaser, I tried very hard with my crayon drawings, and it seemed important to be especially curious about whether the little dolls she placed in my lap were wearing knickers. In those sessions I drew as if my life depended on it. I drew forests seething with all manner of creatures and I made up a complicated bubble-family of rainbow-filled characters. I drew wild deserts and used up all the precious gold crayons for sand dunes, and wasted all the browns on engorged cacti, which seemed to irritate the doctor at the end of our first session.

'Ruby, what if another little girl or boy wanted the gold crayons for their special drawing and they were all used up? Just think how very sad they might feel.'

And the way she looked at me at that moment made me feel more wretched and ashamed than anything else up to this point in my life, even more ashamed than that time I ended up peeing on Mrs Henderson's yellow welcome mat in Reception because I couldn't unstrap my dungarees in time. At the end of the sessions at the clinic I would place my array of paintings on the floor for inspection and the doctor would stand up quickly, peer over my shoulder, turn her head this way and that, weighing up, and then select a few to take away with her. Once, she tilted her head to the side for a long while whilst I waited in the silence, and she took nothing at all. I was free to go home with the pile of rejected papers, which now disgusted me just as much as the dirty gum-flecked carpet they rested on.

Soon afterwards I began having night terrors accompanied by wetting my bed, though I had apparently been a dry girl from an early age. My parents got scared and withdrew me from the sessions. My symptoms quickly disappeared, to their great relief: it was bad enough that their daughter was a dumb mute; a deranged, incontinent mute would have been a step too far.

KITTENS

My mother stared into the basket and blew gently onto the kitten's face. She disturbed its whiskers, but otherwise the little cat's eyes remained firmly closed, as if it was fast asleep. The kitten was unmistakably dead.

Rania began to sob when she saw poor Betty. In her mind there was no doubt as to how the kitten had died. It had died of a broken heart. Rania had pleaded with my parents that she might be allowed to have Betty with her in her bedroom at night, but they were adamant. Animals were not for sleeping with. We were lucky enough to have a furry-pet, and how many Indians did we know who had furry-pets? None. Only Mr Hafiz who owned Baba's butcher's shop had a dog for security, but he was a guard dog, who lived rain or shine in his special kennel outdoors, and even then, the animal had bitten a chunk out of Mrs Hafiz's hand because she forgot to feed him once.

I tried not to think of the noises Betty would have made in her last moments alive and all alone. I am sure she would have tried looking or calling for us. Rania cradled the little dead kitten in her arms and rocked her like a baby.

'You're all glad the kitten's dead,' she cried. My mother fiddled with her sewing then tapped her palms together.

'We can exchange it,' she said, finally. 'We can go and see if Mrs Teasdale has any more kittens left today, if you like, we can go after school, we can go see if there are any left.' My mother continued on like this and Rania began to cry with renewed intensity. She did not want a new kitten – she wanted Betty. She wanted Betty not to be dead. Rania lifted her up and held the stiff ball of fur in her lap but quickly returned her to the basket; it just didn't feel like Betty anymore.

FIRST PERSON

The first person in the world I didn't want to die was a boy who lived at the end of Mitcham Drive: David Girdleston, with the ancestral nose, who once took my hand in a museum. He had the smallest, whitest hands, like the classical statues dotted around the hall gallery.

At lunchtime in the museum we sat on a bench together and I passed him a rubber from my pencil case; he began to erase the sketchy outlines I had been drawing, and then reshaped the sides of my volcano. He drew slowly, curling his fingers tightly round the top of a pencil like a toddler using chubby chalk. His mother worked in the biscuit factory, he told me as he added orange to the tips of the flames, his strokes fine and even. He was abandoned in Heathrow as a sick baby and had a tracheotomy scar to prove it. At night he was pinched awake by all manner of things, including his real mother called Ester and his blood sisters. He offered me his neck and it was true; a faint 'O' spread out like the sun's corona below his Adam's apple.

'You can touch it, I don't mind,' he said.

I hesitated, but it was a gift that might never be given again. So I did feel its delicate outline with just my two fingers, and it was not hard but soft and felt like a raised seam inside a dress.

David lived only yards away from our house and visited often. One time I was visiting David and he said, 'Come and meet Great-Aunt Maggie,' steering me into the living room.

Sitting in the corner was a grand woman wearing complicated, unmatching knitwear and big chunky rings on her fingers with different coloured stones, some as big as toadstools. She'd made a lot of effort with her eye makeup, the dark purple strokes on her lids almost matching her woollen cardigan.

'Come here, come here, bring her to me. Is this the one who doesn't speak?' She addressed this question to David, but I didn't mind really, I was happy to be up close to this woman who smelt sweet and strange and unthreatening.

'Yes, she doesn't speak, Auntie Maggie, but she can hear you very well.'

'She doesn't speak in the Indian?'

'No, Auntie, not even in the Indian.'

'And does she have a tongue?'

'She definitely does, Auntie,' said David, turning around and winking at me.

'I'll pray one for her just in case,' the woman said, unconvinced.

'We'll thank the Lord now,' she said loudly at dinner, taking the chair at the head of the table.

Just before this, in his mother's kitchen, David had kissed me, his hot little tongue meeting my tongue, his hand gripping my wrist about my bare pulse. He reached for a jar on the shelf and carefully placed a clove in my mouth – 'Like little Jesus,' he said – though by then I was old enough not to believe it.

EENA

Mad Eena. Mad Eena had not always been mad. Once upon a time she was just Eena who was retired and before that according to my mother she was Eena who had been given a little silver tray memento from the local maternity ward for delivering more babies in a year than any other midwife. Both my parents knew Eena before-before and were protective of her memory. Unfortunately, it was difficult for my sister and me to remember her any other way. Now Eena is only allowed on supervised outings; sometimes she escapes and is seen, with her cloud of white hair and blue watery eyes that are desperate, looking for something that cannot be found. She waited for me behind the bushes and grabbed my hand and wrenched my body towards her and said:

'Do you seek the heavenly pearl, the godly pearl spoken in Matthew 13:45–46?' I looked into her pale eyes, scared. I nodded my head slowly. 'Good girl, good girl.' Then she loosened her grip and wandered off down the garden.

It felt as if Eena had given me a gift, imparted something vital and important that I might not understand in my tender years but might need later on. I wrote it down when I was back in my room. She had gifted me a parable, a very powerful talisman-like object. It seemed to me that there was a lot to be learned from parables, that they could teach you life skills and give you a way of being. You had to look underneath the words of Jesus – a pearl was not just a pearl – and you had to look beyond the savage jungle of the Bible stories, of Samson slaying his enemies with a poor donkey's freshly killed jawbone. I thought if I concentrated hard enough and shut out all the other noises around me, I could let Jesus and all the other gods in the world inside, and I too could write parables. It fast became a little hobby of mine.

The gods visited me at annoying, unexpected times, when I was not ready for them at all. When I asked I did not receive, and when I least expected them they arrived with no effort. I took to carrying a pen in the elastic of my knickers and would write them down, on my arms, little aphorisms like, 'The tree opens and closes, and we never hear it,' or, 'Even the shiny body of a worm travels with the Lord.'

Occasionally I enlisted David's help, as I knew if he did it, he would be very careful and precise. 'I can do this for you Ruby, trust me, I can write it on you, make it look really nice,' he reassured me, scrutinising the paper. At some point it became very hard to write on my midriff, my little breasts interfered, and I was still of pre-pubescent age where breasts were not be trifled with. Slowly David and I would begin our quiet ceremony – I would stretch the skin on my torso taut as canvas on a frame and he would feed the tip of the pen and copy the patterns and the curlicued script and when his mouth was very near my navel I would touch the top of his hair lightly with my hand.

All good things end, and it came to a head one day as Matilda in gym class put up her hand in the changing rooms – 'Excuse me, Miss Hunt, Ruby is poisoning her blood with her pen' – and then Miss Hunt took me to another room and had a careful look at my parables. I thought she might have read them at least, and gained a little depth and insight, but all she said was, 'No, Ruby, no – this won't do at all. You need to find ways to control your imagination.'

The Eena we knew liked Frosties cereal, malt loaf and mushroom soup out of a tin. Being in Eena and Alf's kitchen was like stepping into a foreign TV show without the subtitles or the sultry, high-cheekboned women. Their kitchen had the smell of old boiled eggs overladen with the smell of dark tobacco smoke, and there was another smell I couldn't reach, maybe because when you are young you haven't smelt all the things you are going to smell yet. There were rumours of a small dog no one had seen that was being kept in the house, and I kept an eye out for the creature, but didn't come upon it on this occasion. The kitchen was originally painted in a bright yellow. The walls were very dirty now but shiny, glossy, and there were raised brownish marks flecking the surface like little raisins. I didn't know if they were dead flies or even bits of desiccated meat, and I didn't want to touch anything. A pair of tall deckchairs were set up and a transistor radio between them emitted some sort of music from a bygone era.

Eena perked up when she saw me. She had been busy in a grubby, over-lit corner, her body hunched over something. She had a plate and offered me an object.

'Have a corned beef rollie. Go on, have two if you like.'

I lifted my hands out of the pockets of my trousers and reached forward reluctantly to take the thing, which resembled a small sausage roll, and placed it in my mouth and began to chew. Under the thin pastry was something masquerading as meat. I chewed and chewed some more; some of the pastry flakes got stuck in my braces but that was the least of my problems. The wobbly mince refused to buckle under the pressure of my tongue. I knew what I was experiencing in that kitchen was a grown-up food dilemma — I must either spit out the fatty bolus and upset old Eena or swallow it and risk gagging and suffocating. I grew hot and flushed.

I took a gamble and made an attempt to swallow it, but my stomach resisted. Eena was trying to hand me a little box that had probably lived on her dressing table for many years. Eena liked to give us presents. We weren't allowed to keep them, mostly, as they tended to be mundane household objects that she and Alf might want to use again: blue-patterned gravy boats, a bedpan, once an old-fashioned ironing board.

'We should sell them to a museum,' said Rania, before my mother made us take them back. But this gift looked as if she had carefully thought it out. It was square and covered in a very heavy silver wrap, with a tiny ancient nail to secure the foil.

'You wind it up clockwise, dearie, and it plays a little ditty you can dance to; even little brown girls can dance to it.' She smiled and I smiled back nervously into her open pale face. I gave her my brightest smile and was trying to back out of the kitchen, sweating, thinking.

Fortunately, the moon was alive and bright that night. I waited till I found a drain down the side alley of the house, whereupon I laid my silver gift on the step and vomited into the drain.

GARDENS

My mother told me I would happily eat bluebells and other abundant spring flowers when I was a toddler. I would chew on their leaves though they were known to be toxic and eventually spit them out and push the mess into a little hollowed-out pocket in a tree. Then I would make a wish. I don't remember doing this or why, but my mother seemed to think it was to attract birds with a soft ready-made nest, and she interpreted this as an early sign of an excess of sensitivity.

SATIN

Once my mother had an accident (moonlight, secateurs) when I was a toddler and there's not much to say about it except some of me remembers and some of me does not. There were striped curtains, floor-length with vertical panels of cream and chocolate satin. They were soft and silky, and I liked to press my cheek against the wide band. The curtains were hung above a radiator, so the lining was always warm, and it felt safe, until it wasn't.

Now that I know planting by moonlight is a thing it makes more sense, and I've pieced it together in a bric-a-brac fashion. According to folklore, root vegetables will start singing in the moonlight, and this is the best time to tend to them. These are the things I've collected together over the years:

- An aborted scream
- A scared-looking bird on a mound of wet leaves
- A used, flipped-over mattress inside a garage

Though this might be part of another memory – I am not always sure.

YOLK

Rania was born with an innie; her belly button has steep sides and a deep crevice. Once she tried to fry an egg on the hottest sunshine day – she lay down on a patio table and seasoned her skin with olive oil, and someone carefully cracked the egg onto her stomach. The cold white dribbled along her waist but the yolk, perfectly balanced, sat glistening in the hollow of her navel. Someone took a photograph. My sister is a talker by the way. Not only that but she's a natural blagger. She's also what I would call a relatable human being.

I have an outie; mine has untidy sides and is shaped like a volcano and probably wouldn't support an egg.

SPRING-BLOOMING BULBS

There's a bit of film that exists of our family in a garden. I am wearing a royal-blue romper suit with white piping, my hair in lopsided bunches. I am trying to blow bubbles. A hand – my mother's, I think – is in view, passing me the wand, which I initially try to put straight into my mouth. She helps me dip and blow, dip and blow. I am inept at this simple task and becoming increasingly frustrated, then Rania makes her perfect debut on a purple tricycle, playing for the camera as she smiles, dismounts and takes the wand and the bottle and blows out beautiful, voluptuous bubbles. I am watching her with baffled concentration. I'm jabbering away in this film, I am not making language with any precision but uttering sounds just fine, no hesitation, no hint of a stutter, my clever two-year-old self.

It was my sister's words that used to come out so quickly, in a torrential rush, that it was difficult to understand her in the early days. I was the only one who could translate her jumbled speech. All of the words would collapse backwards on themselves or come out in one effervescent stream until she eventually slowed down.

Sometimes I could see my mother turning her gaze from one daughter to the other, and I could almost hear the voices competing in her head. Some nights my sister and I would work our way quietly to the landing radiator where we would absorb the last of its heat and gently eavesdrop. My father, who's always seen the glass half full even when it's down to its last miserable dregs, would say, 'Things could be worse, Jaan.' (He always calls her this when they are absolutely alone.) 'We need to have some perspective.' This is my father's favourite word in the whole world. 'See, it could be worse: they are both healthy, growing girls; look at Arun's twins, born so early and all their problems, and Tina's daughter born with that birthmark cursed over the entire side of her face so she can barely open that eye, all these operations . . . '

'Oh yes, yes, Dilip,' she interrupts (she doesn't have a pet name for him). 'We are very lucky, this country is very auspicious – I should count my blessings that we all have our fingers and toenails and noses on our faces.' Then she'll poke her hands in her hair to retrieve her hairgrips and we hear them tinkle onto the little enamel tray on her bedside table, then she'll laugh a little, then a bit too much and a bit too loudly, and Rania will begin to stroke my back, and my father will slink a little deeper into the bedclothes.

BEFORE

My parents met the neighbours. On the right, Eena and Alfred Parker; on the left, at Number 14, were the Indians, the Panesars. A Sikh family.

'They are from the Jat caste and not like us,' said my mother.

'You don't think anyone is like us,' pointed out my father.

'And you think everyone is like us: the sweepers of the street, they are like us . . . the English even they are also like us, I suppose?'

After their initial shy introductions, Eena's eyes rested on my mother's bulging belly. The following week she delivered three packs of booties and speedily knitted a shawl in yellow wool.

The children came. My sister Rania was late, but my mother managed to push her out with surprisingly little effort in the maternity wing in Central Middlesex.

'She will be called Rania,' my mother said, decisively. Dilip opened his mouth and shut it again, slightly taken aback by how quickly my mother was losing her meek expression of acquiescence.

My mother's pregnancy with me was not an easy one – the enervating heat of August, combined with a toddler who demanded her constantly, sapped all her precious energy.

She presented breech, and so was subject to uncomfortable manipulations by the hands of a bossy midwife who attempted to turn the baby. But baby-me remained resolute and unmovable. The doctors began to talk of C-sections and forceps. Bossy Midwife Number Two was dispatched and asked to shave the mother's private parts and my mother began to weep.

'Don't worry! You know Julius Caesar was cut out from his mother's belly,' said my father.

'No, he wasn't!' my mother contradicted, as she had always been an attentive student, particularly in Mr Verma's classical history lessons. 'Julius Caesar was not cut out of his poor suffering mother, it's a myth.'

The baby did come my mother's way, but not only was I feet-first, I also had the cord wrapped around my neck, twice for luck. Also, I was a crier. All babies cry but I seemed to cry all the time. With my sister it had been an easy age-old pattern – Rania would cry, my mother would fasten her to the nipple, she would fall asleep and then would feed again a couple of hours later. At night she would fall asleep with her baby at her breast, and the baby would find and suck her nipple any time at her leisure. The two of them would perform this dance till presumably my mother's milk changed flavour, or Rania became bored of the dance, and one day jumped off the bed and walked away from my mother's breast towards the fridge. But nothing in the world would settle me.

My mother was attended by a health visitor who was suspicious about Indian mothers and their baby-mother-habits, and although my mother seemed compliant, Linda Norton suspected that she ignored her advice when her back was turned, resorting to herbs and powders to alleviate colic symptoms and teething. The health visitor wrote up in her report that she was of the opinion that my mother had applied unsterile chappati dough to her breasts in an attempt to cure severe bouts of mastitis. My father, who has always been the curious sort and could never resist an open book, peeped at the notes whilst her back was turned and she was weighing little me on her scales. He threw the appalling Mrs Norton out of the house.

GARDENS

My mother discovered the garden, or the garden discovered her. Whichever way round, it all started the morning of the lost pacifier and my post-Farley's Rusks vomiting. My mother quickly stuffed her feet into my father's outdoor shoes, and with a kitchen utensil still tightly held in her hand like a weapon she pushed open the back door and went to cry into the weeds next to the falling-down shed. She heard a clear male voice.

'You won't get it rid of that way, love.'

She arched her head around the shed. Mr Parker was sitting on a stripy sagging deckchair, puffing on his pipe.

'Good-morning-Mr-Parker-nice-to-see-you-lovely-weather.' She said this quickly, in as normal a way as possible, hoping he wouldn't notice her ridiculous footwear or the wooden spatula congealed with rice.

Mr Parker used his stick to ease himself up, stood and pointed down to where she was standing.

'That there is ground elder, you got a nasty carpet of it going. It's fast-growing and vicious, but I wouldn't bother with any of those chemicals if that's what you're thinking.'

My mother began to focus on the man in front of her. He was tall and burly with tiny little glasses. He wore braces clipped onto his wide trousers.

His garden-talk sounded very serious.

'Well, they say . . . that it's best, with ground elder, to pull it out little and often, a bit like dusting.'

He pulled up a few of the knotty root's strands.

'See, if you do that when you can, and maybe every few days or few weeks you go in with a hoe – that might make a difference. Just be careful of the wisteria nearby and those roses.'

Alfred Parker must have studied this strange woman in front of him; she had the longest, thickest rope of hair he had ever seen, such black hair and such black eyes.

'I most certainly will, Mr Parker,' she said again with a stronger voice.

Unused to such a captive audience Mr Parker stretched his legs and got into his stride. He extemporised on the world of plants, fertiliser, greenfly spray, herbaceous borders and begonias.

Whilst Mr Parker spoke, he would now and then break off for a long suck on his pipe; it transmitted a heavy but not unpleasant reassuring smell that lingered and made my mother a little woozy.

Roses. Wisteria. Ground elder. My mother opened up her ears and listened. When she re-entered the house her equilibrium was restored, and she had already decided where to plant her first potatoes, and how to maintain a good soil texture, and she was going to find out what a well-balanced hoe was and acquire one immediately. She was going to tackle that ground elder that was nothing but a common garden thug from the sound of things.

Under Mr Parker's guidance her own garden came to life. She mowed, she weeded, she plucked, and then she hoed, seeded and watered. Mr Parker encouraged her to use his greenhouse, so her precious seedlings gentled in the warmth until they were ready to be transplanted. She even persuaded my father to pay someone to press the lawn with a roller.

My mother had to come to terms with the fact that the rest of her family showed no interest in or any gift for green living things. My father feigned an interest but really his heart was not in it. One would think plants would be easier than flesh-covered humans, but too many people are afraid of getting the names wrong, of taking responsibility for something that lives in unpredictable conditions. My mother is an indirect talker; she talks through her hands. If her hands were full of her skein of knitting, or she was tinkering with the bell peppers in the garden, talk ran out of her like rain.

When I was younger, I used to stay close to her side in the garden; I would set up a little stool and listen to my mother talk about nothing and everything. Later in the day I would pick up my stool and gravitate towards Mr Parker's garden. He never asked me a single thing but was content to sit and talk about the moon landings and the Nixon tapes and about all the tools and implements he'd used over the years to do battle with the foxes. That was the one thing that he and my mother would never agree on. My mother didn't mind the foxes, despite the harm they did – tearing big holes in the lawn – and the sharp musky smell of their shit. She went looking for them, fed them secretly, she felt for their babies.

I REMEMBER

After school, a park . . . pigeons, and a bench with metal scrolled arms. I am wearing a skirt, the bench slats digging into my legs, so instead I am sitting on my hands waiting for Rania, who's high on top of the new roundabout, a Witch's Hat, on the highest rung, her hair flung back.

I remember a dog I was scared of and wanting to run and my sister shouting, 'Don't run, Ruby, don't run,' from the top of her perch, but I took flight . . . I ran anyway . . . my school satchel bumping at my hip, *thwack*, *thwack* on the jointed bone, and the dog chasing and barking at my side and Rania jumping off and landing on her knee, the patella shattering like a walnut, the sound of her scream, a high pure scream of distilled pain and the yellow dog's owner was at her side, the dog captured and tied to a stump and Rania crying and grabbing me by the wrist.

'I told you not to run, Ruby, you silly girl. You stupid, dumb girl, Ruby.' The wet feeling on the back of my thighs. I'd been bitten by the Alsatian – but *had* I been bitten, or had I passed water?

Where was Mum? I didn't know. I remember my mother earlier, in a blue tunic with white flowers, standing under a bright, golden-haired tree which I now know to be mimosa.

I thought I saw her flickering like a candle under the mimosa for a few seconds. She was there, I thought, and then she was gone.

ANGELS

I went into hospital when I was nine. I was lifted out of my body and I floated up to the ceiling and looked down at my nine-year-old self, a birdlike figure on the pillow, the exact same face as mine but more vulnerable.

I looked at my sleeping girl-self from up where I floated, I thought from almost every angle how truly pathetic she looked, perhaps because her eyes were softly closed. Was this truly all I was made up of? I made the decision to stay there a while longer, despite the indefatigable pull, that strong-willed force, from little me lying asleep on the bed. It was like a sad soap opera. The doctors went in and out, the nurses kept taking blood from a tap in my arm. My mother was crying, my father was crying, but he was also holding my bluebird hair clips in his hand (so that's where they went).

Nothing hurt, incidentally; my body was somewhat cooler, nothing mattered, time didn't matter, up there. The minute I awoke I looked up at the ceiling to check for the other Ruby, but she must have been back inside me now. Nothing was so certain anymore, though; the colours around me resisted then returned unrushingly, the sounds in the ward retuned themselves, the hospital bed with its heavy, white, cold sheets, the curtains with the cartoon world maps – everything was buzzing, my heart was definitely beating and I turned to the nurse and mouthed *ice cream.*

When they got me home, they put me in the huge king-size bed, and my mother began to sleep with me. First, she prepared the room by spraying it with a special flower essence, and then plumped my pillows, whilst I sat marooned in their bed in a quilted bedjacket like a large china doll.

Though I was cured of one disease another one exchanged places with it. The first time I was ill all the talk was about virus-related elevated liver enzymes and organ stress. Now my vital organs had recovered perfectly and this time it was my legs. They refused to obey me and refused to walk. In fact they were drained of feeling as if the cartilage and bones had somehow mysteriously dissolved. The doctors put it down to a combination of psychological distress and post-viral fatigue. Inexplicably the hair on my legs grew longer, it was extraordinary to see the hair, it seemed to be growing like grass. I was exhilarated by my new-found hairiness. Rania took a look at my legs and compared and contrasted the soft and wispy leg hair on her own shins. 'Yours is so dense, more like fur,' she concluded after stroking my hair in the opposite direction to its nap. 'Imagine if it just grew and grew and later you could plait it and comb it and make wigs from it.' I slapped away her hand and pulled down my nightie to my toes. I became quite protective about my leg hair after that and wore long pyjamas and decided I was humbled by my little body trying its best to hide the shame of my skinny misbehaving legs.

What I discovered was we can manage without legs for a short time. I crawled everywhere: from my bedroom to the bathroom, from the linoleum to the garden patio area. It's amazing what the other parts of your body will do to compensate and in no time I had learned to shuffle then glide not inelegantly along the kitchen floor.

During this episode we had a visitor in our house; Biji had just arrived from India. My mother's mother was born to the business of healing and was blessed with exceptional curative powers; she had never really wanted to come to England in the first place but now it was obvious her special gifts were needed. First she passed an object over my legs: a stick with dark wooden beads on one end, which resembled warm eggs, and it was so delicious I even let out a low moan in pleasure which was mistaken for pain.

Just a few days later somehow she had arranged for a hakim to visit the house. Biji ushered him into my bedroom and he asked me to cough into a handkerchief. The pensive old man put on his glasses and studied the piece of cloth, opened his satchel and handed Biji ten tiny pieces of folded paper, each of which contained bitter white powders. Rania told me she stole one to verify its contents and that it tasted of Fun Dip cut with a bit of lime. 'It's a placebo, Ruby, it's to trick you into being cured, you see?'

Everyone was very reverential, and the visitors spoke in hushed tones. My classmates had made me a huge card and everyone had signed it including the boys and even the twins

Mia and Tia signed it in their odd strangulated script. On the card a big red ruby had been imaginatively sprinkled with red glitter, and Mrs O'Donovan had thoughtfully composed a little poem, with 'Ruby' half-rhyming with 'truly'. It was propped up next to me on the bedside table and began to slowly shed its glitter on the carpet, revealing the thick lines of the drawn heart, bald and exposed, till the whole thing looked so sad that I had to wrap it up in newspaper and throw it away.

All the neighbours' children and parents came to visit bearing gifts of comics and variety biscuit boxes and David from across the road brought my favourite Hoop crisps. I was the unwalking, untalking, uncomplaining miracle.

My mother settled me on her hip and we ventured out into the garden like this, I was pressed very close to her body, my lower limbs dangling like rag doll legs whilst she meandered around her domain talking all the while. 'Oh Ruby, you are lighter than a cat,' she whispered in my ear; 'Look, Ruby, here,' as she pointed at the soil or brushed her fingers along the crates of spinach. Those days gave me a tantalising glimpse of what my future might hold, how I could so easily retreat into the blank centre of myself forever bathed in the light of all the love of my mother. At night my mother lay alongside me, praying and squeezing juice through my lips.

'The problem is that Ruby likes it too much,' said Auntie Number One to Rania following another afternoon spectacle where they watched my mother gently carrying me to the garden with a cloudy pink shawl on my back.

'Ruby will be rocking in a cot and we'll be changing her nappy like a bloody newborn baby if she carries on like this,' said Rania to Auntie Number One. By now there was even talk of homeschooling and pooling resources with Mr Martin's daughters who were Jehovah's and didn't believe in traditional education.

Auntie Number One intervened and arranged for a real doctor to visit. He took one look at the situation and simply applied logic to the task. He sent everyone away and ceremonially washed his hands with his own medicine soap and dried them meticulously on a lint-free towel.

'Now, Miss Ruby, shall we stop this game, entertaining as it is?' He said this kindly to me whilst holding my shin. 'Let's talk, shall we. Or you can listen at least?' I was by then more than ready to listen, my mother was loosening, seeing less of her needy daughter, she was missing meals and floating around and disappearing upstairs and had even stopped sleeping in our bed.

'I give Mum till the end of the week,' I heard Rania say several times because if you say the worst thing out loud it can stop it happening. Auntie Number One tried to give her a hug but Rania made a face and ignored her. The next morning my father had rung the emergency number from the card in his pocket and by the evening she was gone again. The day after that my legs came back.

Afterwards Biji says, 'This demonstrates that God is most of the time sleeping and sometimes you have to gently stir him and force him to reveal his hand.'

'You shouldn't have to wake him,' says Rania, 'he should be awake all the time and I don't believe in God and if there was a God, I don't think that he is good.'

'What you are saying is the opposite of good. God is good.' Biji raises her voice a fraction.

Auntie Number One has been quiet but then coughs when our father enters the room.

'God has got us into this situation in the first place,' continues Rania.

'I don't follow you,' says my father distractedly. He's stopped in the middle of the room directly under the ceiling rose light and seems both illuminated and lost.

'God is dead,' says Rania emphatically.

'What? Who is dead?' repeats my father.

'God is dead,' she says louder. 'God is dead!'

'Stop it now, he might hear you,' says Biji.

'You just said he was asleep so make up your mind.'

My father doesn't move. I hold my breath and begin to count the clusters of orange-yellow flowers on the wallpaper behind him. I don't want to think of God asleep gently snoring with his old God mouth not hearing the pink baby birds dropping out of their nests. If he made them why doesn't he save them?

By now my father has covered his face and he is crying, his shoulders shaking up and down. I want Rania to stop.

'God is dead,' she says again. 'God is dead.'

MOONLIGHT, SECATEURS

The night of the accident my very beautiful mother refused to leave the garden. Mr Parker tried to persuade her to come in first. Rania and I were watching from the window upstairs, we couldn't hear them talking, but my mother remained with her hands in the soil kneeling on her cushion. Mr Parker shook his head sadly and headed back to his kitchen. My father tried some more, he even tried to lift her up but she remained planted there firmly. Every now and then she would reach into the pocket of her long cardigan, the fragile armour she always wore in the garden, and pop a shelled nut into her mouth for sustenance. Some more hours passed and still she was at it, her legs must have been numb with cold, all the neighbours were watching from a distance, the light was poor outside, and someone fetched the torches. Eventually I fell asleep but not for long and I woke in someone's lap, everything smelt different, I hadn't brushed my teeth and I was thirsty and began to cry. Someone picked me up and placed me on the sofa, but I was wide awake now and there was a crowd in the garden. I stole my way onto the patio. 'Just come in,' my father was pleading to my mother, 'it's so late, it's so cold, and you must be hungry.' My mother didn't appear to be listening. Her gloveless hands were poking the borders. I wanted to see my mother's face. I wanted to ask her why she didn't like our house anymore but then the visitors arrive quietly, they stand like giant spectral trees and surround her. 'We are here to help you,' they say to her, 'we are here to take care of you, there's no need to be afraid,' but they say this at the same time as stalking her, their sleeves rolled up ready to capture and throw her into a big wide sack. One of them grabs my mother's arm and pulls her forward, she places her hand deep into a pocket and out comes a pair of scissors, I scream, my mother screams, there's blood on her hands, blood varnishing the leaves in the moonlight.

BANGLES

'I know, we could make one,' says Rania on the sixth day I wouldn't stop crying. It was the holidays, we were on the settee with our feet up, under blankets, and it hadn't stopped raining since the accident. I had barely slept. Every time I closed my eyes I saw her face through the torchlight and when I opened them again shadows flicked around my room like dark, oversized flies. My thoughts were beginning to become as soft and spongy as the garden grass and then finally Rania had this idea. She pulled me upstairs. We went into my mother's wardrobe and opened the door. Rania reached for the hangers and the shoes on the floor and laid them out on the bedroom carpet. 'Look,' said Rania, and I stopped rubbing at my eyes and saw what Rania was doing. Rania had laid out the burgundy trousers and tunic and added a scarf and so I went to the dressing table and found the red velvet-lined box and carefully extracted the thin gold bangles and placed them at the end of the sleeves.

I remember now how we both used to climb into her wardrobe and sit in the bedlam of clothes at the bottom, inhale deeply, and feel all at once a peace and calm.

'There. All better now?' said Rania, smiling. We both lay down on either side. I clutched a sleeve. I knew it wasn't the real thing but it was something and I closed my eyes and sucked hard at my thumb and fell asleep sweetly till my father came home and lifted me to bed.

FATHER

My father was an untidily put-together man with a mild temperament. He was short and spent too much of his time scratching his head, trying to understand all the women in his life. His own father had died young. His mother and his six sisters ruled the roost. His parents had been tall, and all his sisters, who cursed their height, also towered over him. 'But a beautiful thing is never perfect,' my father would say. His own wife defeated him entirely, as did each of his daughters, first Rania and then me. Nothing else was beyond his realm of understanding – he really should have been a scholar. When he was relaxed, my father's tongue would loosen as he would carefully angle his glass and pour his beer.

'O Thestorides, of the many things hidden from the knowledge of man, nothing is more unintelligible than the human heart!'

In family emergencies he had been known to quote Socrates, Bruce Lee, Muhammad Ali, and sometimes he would let a little Gandhi in, though deep down we all knew he preferred the classics.

My mother mulched the vegetable patch and withdrew from the earth her first crop of firm, silky-skinned aubergines, followed closely by yellow peppers and tomatoes when she finally got the hang of blight resistance.

49

MANJU

My parents had a friend that sometimes came around who we called Auntie Manju. She was always dressed in a sari, though she wore it in such a dishevelled fashion that it defeated the point of wearing something that's supposed to be draped elegantly around and around your body. On the occasions she visited, my mother used to dispense with the usual long introduction to her children and race her past us into the living room and then shut the door. Sometimes we used to press our ears to the wall, or Rania would go in on some imaginary mission, but we were shooed away. One time I walked into the room and I wish I hadn't. Auntie Manju was sitting in the middle of the room crying and rocking back and forth in my mother's arms.

Once I was asked to give Manju a glass of tepid water in the garden. She was sitting on the bench looking so lost and sad and I inched towards her with the glass on the tray, and she took the glass of water but tested it first on her elbow like mothers do with milk before they give the warmed bottle to their infants. I never found out what happened to Auntie Manju's babies. Were they dead and if so, how did they die? Were they taken away from her or did the hospital take them away because of Manju's madness? What came first – the madness or the babies?

'Please tell us why Manju is mad,' pleaded Rania. My mother told us that there is common madness, and then there is a mother's madness. The kind afflicting Auntie Manju was the latter kind and she would not be rid of it till the day she died. 'One day,' continued my mother, 'Auntie Manju must quietly resign herself to her fate. She must stop blaming her husband and his relatives, she must put down her weapons, and greet her madness like a familiar ghost.' I listened to my mother telling us the story about Manju, and then it was finished and I thought we had been short-changed. I wanted a moral in the story, something I could take away and learn from, but my mother would say no more, and drifted into silence as she began plaiting her long hair, still damp from her bath.

The truth is, I never thought about my mum being mad like Manju until David mentioned it one day in passing. We were at his house after school and sharing a giant packet of crisps in his bedroom.

David had an unhealthy obsession with spiders. He liked to stalk and trap them and keep them as pets. He was making a system of bridges in the corner of his room, in the hope they might be entertained, but these creatures had anarchic tendencies and would spoil his fun by fleeing behind the radiator or refusing to leave the matchboxes he was housing them in.

'I heard your mother was in a mad asylum,' he started to say. I knew I didn't have a name for what my mum was exactly, but it wasn't that. Manju was mad with baby sickness and Eena next door was mad with an old-age sickness, but my mum was not that kind of mad. I tipped the crisps over David's head and ran home.

David ran after me. 'Sorry, sorry, Ruby, I didn't mean to hurt your feelings, come back and I'll make it up to you.'

When I got home I noticed a small house spider was clinging to the elastic of my school sock. I could hear David calling for me, shouting through the letterbox. I wondered about forgiveness. 'If your brother or sister sins against you, rebuke them, and if they repent, forgive them,' he says, repeating one of my lines he must have memorised from scrawling on my stomach. Rania enters the room.

'You can hear him, right? That silly friend of yours? Shall I get rid of him?'

I don't turn around, I am too close to tears, but I nod my head. His words had punched a little hole in my heart. That's the thing with words; they flit out of your mouth into the air, there's no going back once they're out.

In the life I've led so far I've learned certain things, some vitally important and some not: camels' blood cells are oval, and not doughnut-shaped like ours; not all mothers in the animal kingdom are good; rabbits eat their babies; Jesus doesn't always love you.

AGONY

When I first heard the word agony from the mouth of my mother I was halfway up the stairs and it had escaped from underneath my parents' bedroom door. It was as if some unknown force had passed me on the staircase; I felt winded and had to quickly grab hold of the bannister to steady myself.

Of all the 'a' words, agony is the worst. I wouldn't wish that word on my greatest enemy. I wasn't even that sure what the word meant but it was clear to me there was a sliver of glass in the middle of the brittle 'o'. Agony was the point of no return, no greater anguish could befall you when reached it, and there was no coming back from the edge of its abyss — which was another 'a' word.

DREAMS

My father is climbing. In his dream he is climbing, but it seems that only God knows where he is climbing to. Nowhere he has ever been, but a place that is faintly familiar: the smell of diesel from below, concentrated dog piss from the corners of the stairwells. He is somewhere like a city, perhaps from an American film he might have seen, one of those films where a tower is burning, an inferno and there are only stairs, but no. He is not going *down* the stairs in his dream – he is going *up* those stairs. My father is by nature a hopeful man – that was the cloth he was cut from, and his father before that – his ancestral cloth is steeped in hope. But this is not a very hopeful dream.

My father. No one can quite match his sartorial distinctiveness. In other words, my father dresses like shit. For most people this would present problems but somehow it increases his infantile charm.

My father has a hat he loves to wear, the colour of dark fern. He stands in the hallway mirror and adjusts it to what he calls his jaunty angle.

In the car, we used to play the animal game. The rules were very basic. Rania chose a chimpanzee, which was funny at the time because she had learned how to climb out the bedroom window and walk across the sloped roof of the kitchen to the safety of the patio area. I chose a mouse, just because it was easier, and if I'd chosen a dolphin (the animal I really wanted) Rania would have reminded me that the point of the game was to think of the animal you were most like, not the animal you most aspired to be. Everyone seemed content with me arriving at the mouse as my spirit animal even though I had no affinity with a mouse or any rodents whatsoever. My father saw himself as an elephant. A predictable choice. A dependable animal who displays clear signs of humanlike empathy. An animal that holds extravagant funerals for its loved ones. But I don't believe my father is an elephant; he is most like a canary. His main role in our family is to detect early signs of disturbance and then to flap his wings and warble a little. Of course, usually no one takes notice, or if they notice it's too late, but that isn't, strictly speaking, the canary's fault.

'Let's choose one for your mother,' he said. 'Let's choose her an animal.' But neither Rania nor I wanted to choose an animal for her. We didn't think it was right. If she wanted an animal, she needed to get better and choose her animal herself.

MUGS

When the garden's asleep for winter, when there's nothing to nurture, nothing to fight for or revive on the borders, when my mother has put away her tools and potting soil in our shed, that strange look of blank hunger takes up residence. These are the beginnings of Mugdays. Mugdays start with unpredictable and approximate mornings. Simple things, like getting out of bed and into some fresh clothes, eating and drinking, have to be gently negotiated, navigated and pleaded for.

My father reverts to martial metaphors like 'champ', 'soldier' and 'warrior', which he employs when he's committed to a night shift, when he needs to leave us alone with our mother. Rania as the oldest was 'the night champ', and gets to double-lock the door behind him and take on Mugduty in our parents' bedroom.

During Mugdays, which sometimes extend to Mugweeks, we cling to the simple things. Mostly they are half-things. Half a spoon of breakfast cereal into a half-willing mouth. My father whose glass is always half full clings on to these halves, because we know nothing, really, except that there will be an end. That she will (for reasons as unreachable and mystifying to us as what brought her to Mugdays in the first place) simply wake up one morning and appear in the kitchen fully clothed. Not one of us will say anything, but we'll all sit down at the table together and drink our tea, and lightly try out conversation again. Rania will test a few words in the air. I will watch mother-bird put her hands on the kitchen table, lay them out one at a time, like pieces of delicate lace, and I will breathe very quietly, my knees very close to my mother's but not quite touching, and slowly it will almost begin to feel like a normal family again.

PAINT

The universe began as a small ball and then exploded to its current cosmic dimensions. We have less knowledge than we think. Rania wants all the knowledge.

When we were small and playing with paints, she would startle herself with the brilliant colours.

My mother would say encouraging words and then ask us to stop. I would stop mid-stroke, the brush still in the air, but Rania could not stop. Her fingers would haphazardly brush the paper, and moments later she had smeared the entire surface with black paint and obliterated her early masterpiece.

Later, when Rania progressed to fine brushes, her art teachers would enthuse and then purse their lips with concern: 'Maybe you should stop now, Rania – I think it's perfect as it is,' but Rania pressed on. It's not that she didn't want to stop, but some inexorable force pushed her further to the *what if* at the core of wonder. What if she just added a little more mauve or purple, or what if she added another tree, another clod or cloud?

Her hands worked furiously and purposefully towards some mystical goal, till her beautiful painting was annihilated, ruined by her dark, fitful splurges, the outlines of objects barely decipherable. Rania would stare blankly, survey the ruins, the *what if* answered like the slap of an oceanic wave in her face.

SULTANS

Biji was coming to visit. This distant, faraway person who had raised our mother, and who had always been *over there*, was coming over here, again. Biji arrived and installed herself in the corner of our kitchen. In her lap was a mound of ginger roots; she deftly shredded the peel with a tiny blade whilst simultaneously managing to pop fried lotus seeds into her mouth. When I entered the kitchen, my mother pushed me, not very gently, in her direction, until I was half in her lap of ginger scraps and half in her hefty arms. Biji was a talker. As she talked she pulled me into her, pinched my waist and examined a mole on my neck by twisting it anticlockwise. Much of what she said I couldn't understand in her old-style Punjabi delivered much too fast. She had already put away her things in the bedroom. She was clearly very attached to her suitcase, and rather than empty it she had reorganised it so that it became a serviceable wardrobe. Cohabiting with Biji was actually easier than I thought. Though she spoke incessantly it was more like the gentle pitter-patter of rain on a tin roof – her voice was melodious and punctuated with light scraps of laughter. This is how we used to sleep: at bedtime I would take her heavy glasses from her hands. Then she would lie down on her side facing me and talk. In the half-dark I could make out her moving lips and the sheen in her pupils, but I couldn't be sure if she was actually awake or if it was that her dreams were leaking out of her mouth. Slowly her talk would ease off, until all you could hear was her gentle breath and occasional whistling through her nostrils.

Biji told us the most incredible fables, usually about the families of sultans and all their various adventures and dilemmas, and how they constantly failed their wives.

There was the sultan married to a young princess who was as beautiful as she was wise. The sultan and his wife were very content at first; the kingdom prospered; there were rains and decent harvests. Wars were averted. Every year his wife would deliver a child. After a decade, the couple counted eight children, each perfectly limbed but each one a girl. The sultan ruminated regretfully over his unfortunate circumstances. He began to mourn his lack of sons. On his tours across his kingdom he noticed no shortage of boys and young men. Even his humble cup-bearer grew fat with a dozen sons. The sultan's thoughts grew darker, till his counsellors eventually persuaded him to declare her bewitched. They brought his beautiful wife to a field, and his servants built a wall and roof around her and sealed her in. If she survived it meant the gods had spared her; if she died, she was a witch. Of course, she suffocated inside the walls and he remarried. But each time he saw a koel bird in his gardens he would hear his departed wife speaking from its mouth. *What you did to me was a great wrong, you are a weak man who doesn't deserve a kingdom*, she said. Driven mad, the sultan threw himself into the River of Anguish.

'That's the saddest story I have ever heard,' said Rania. 'Where did you find it?' But I know the answer to that. In its ancient logic, people want shortcuts to happiness, but there are no shortcuts. A bud can't be forced – or rather you can force it but the flower will be sad and will fail to scent. The sultan wouldn't wait patiently. Everything takes its time.

Biji told us she was married to my grandfather when she was ten years of age. Two months after starting to bleed, and not yet fourteen, she was finally taken to her new home. Biji kept her eyes lowered respectfully when she was formally introduced to her husband, but she spent some time inspecting his feet, which she noted were large, pale and unusually hirsute. For some time Biji harboured the belief that her husband was afflicted by some sort of malady of the brain: he named the intimate parts of her body. Her left breast he christened Horatio and the right Tiresias. He was prone to periods of deep contemplation. Later, she realised he had been taught by holy sisters in a Catholic school, so she became a little less concerned. Biji was a talker.

Biji had a vicelike grip on her old certainties. If you complied with certain tenets of behaviour fastidiously and without question, then you could do whatever the hell you wanted with the other parts of your life.

Biji divided food into two hermetically sealed categories: garam (hot foods) and thanda (cold). But these categories, we soon discovered, had absolutely nothing to do with either temperature or chilli content. Instead it had something to do with some secret the very few – the initiated – knew about, some indefinable, immutable characteristic of the food itself. Under Biji's regime my mother was prohibited from eating eggs, lamb, mustard, mushrooms and mango, which were all garam foods.

Biji made hardly any judgements about her grandchildren –
though she decided the girls were too long in the limb, there
was no cure for that now – and she didn't bat an eye when
Rania's friend Felix came into the house wearing a chain in
his ear and eyeliner, his hair gel-stiffed down into a diamond
shape. She chided her daughter, though. How could she
have let us cut our own hair? And as for my fringe? It would
grow down and give me an irreversible hairy forehead like a
monkey . . . like Auntie Naveen, and look at her now: stubborn
as a coconut, hairy as a coconut, unmarried as a coconut.

STRAWS

My father tried various ways of bribing Biji to stay. But she knew her departure date and was immovable. My mother couldn't bear to accompany her to the airport, so my father drove her and the rest of us all waved from the front gate.

After Biji flew off in the aeroplane bits of the house started falling apart in sympathy. We were distracted by the boiler, which stopped working first, and then the doorbell started ringing incessantly, even when we took the batteries out, and our father had to deaden it using a pair of pliers.

I am convinced that Biji booby-trapped the house so we would use up our energies on heating water and washing our hair in the sink.

On the first three days after school there were mango milkshakes on the kitchen table, with striped straws, accompanied by snacks in boat-shaped dishes, and we all ate our food politely with the spirit of the departed Biji all around us.

The fourth day there were no stripy straws, and by the end of day five there were no milkshakes, and my mother had taken to her bed, and my father had hidden the knives.

'Not the scissors too,' moaned Rania.

'They needed sharpening,' said my father, simply.

The day after that, Terrible Auntie Number One arrived.

We found her flitting around our father like a moth. Disasters are when some people come into their own, and Auntie Number One was number one at disaster management.

'She is unmarried and that's why her food is so bad,' said Biji, 'it's tainted by the bitterness of unmarriage and the foul bile that builds up in a barren womb.'

'It's got nothing to do with the fact that she just hates cooking because she has important things — like an actual job — to do,' said Rania.

We disliked Auntie Number One unfairly because she almost always appeared when there was some crisis or other in the family, when we would come home from school and find her in the kitchen, blending superfood smoothies and pretending to like the cats. The name stuck because there was something a little *off* about Auntie Number One. Her two front teeth overlapped. Whenever she bought us presents, they were never quite right: the clothes were a year too small, the vintage toys had a pointless tragic air, even her smoothies missed some vital, unreachable, unidentifiable ingredient.

Rania and I knew the truth about Auntie Number One; we had come across her once on The High Street. We knew she lived with a man; we caught sight of her putting up posters for the Labour Party with someone who wore a leather jacket; they kept leaning into each other and sharing a kiss and a roll-up cigarette. Rania was impressed. 'Look, Ruby, he's not even bad-looking — good for Auntie Number One. She actually seems happy.'

GARDENS

No one could quite remember why there were no fences separating the gardens. No boundaries meant five whole households had the run of them, these gardens that were already so long no lawnmower could reach their wild final third. Only the Parkers looked after theirs properly – they grew azaleas, and planted bulbs at the right time in the year so they flourished in the springtime, and also maintained a compost heap.

Running along the gardens at the back was a two-metre strip of no man's land partitioned off by a fence. Someone had a vague notion that it was owned by the electricity board, or London Transport, but the boundary had fallen into disrepair – an old chain-link fence going to rust, mostly covered with ivy and crawlers rising up from vines around a couple of trees which stood dead at the bottom of the garden. Because the houses were built on an old fruit orchard many trees remained, and the gardens were so overgrown that from the houses it was difficult to get a view of this section of the garden at all.

The first house on the street was where Kirsty Lennard lived. She didn't mix with anyone on the road. She lived there with her mother Maggie and her stepfather Brian, plus his two older boys. There was a whiff of fear hanging around the family, which eased Kirsty's time at school. It wasn't just the brown kids that avoided her – we all steered clear of her two older stepbrothers who were growing out skinheads. Brian ignored his neighbours and had a reputation for being dangerous. Once I heard David's mum say she had been good friends with Brian's first wife, and that Brian had a lot of good in him somewhere if people gave him half a chance.

One summer Rania convinced us all that she had mystic powers and could make predictions by examining birthmarks, or, failing that, facial moles, and she would tell you how you died in your previous life. Rania rimmed her eyes with kajal and floated outside to the garden dressed in my mother's old kimono and my father's old cowboy boots.

Rania got bored after a while and decided she could predict other things too.

Kirsty Lennard decided the temptation was too much and approached Rania.

'Go on then,' she said, 'do my reading.'

Rania appraised the girl. She was thinking quickly. This girl was a hornet. She had seen enough of her to know what she was, but she had a needy vulnerability in her eyes too that Rania hadn't noticed before. Rania shuffled her tarot cards slowly then lit another stick of incense.

'You want to know how you died or how you will die? I can do both.'

'After. The future. I don't care about before.'

Kirsty moved her hair off her shoulders and revealed a coffee-stain mark the size of a giant marble.

Rania took a deep breath and looked intently at the girl.

'Are you sure you want to know? . . . It's not pleasant.' Rania paused for dramatic effect. 'I am afraid you are going to die by your own hand . . . Whenever a neck is marked anywhere near the ear it's always a very clear predictor from the ancients, yes.' Rania tapped her head. 'It will be by hanging most probably.'

Kirsty was trembling.

'You liar – take it back, you fucking bitch,' shouted Kirsty, 'you don't know anything.'

'OK,' said Rania, shrugging, starting to put away her incense and cards. 'I'll take it back. What do I know about anything.'

That evening Brian came to our door.

'Keep that witch of yours away from my stepdaughter,' he said, pushing my father into the hallway. Rania was screaming, 'Get out, get off him,' and punching his back. Brian grabbed both Rania's hands in one fist and had his finger close to her face. 'Don't ever tell me what to do, girl,' he said calmly. Then he left.

Every Saturday Brian and his two sons put up a little table under the horse statue on Bell Corner to hand out pamphlets and sometimes Kirsty was with them. Once we walked past with Auntie Number One and she said: 'These people are more dangerous than bog-standard Paki-bashers; it's the ones with ideas who read books and know about theory and dialectics and use their actual imaginations, they are the ones you really need to watch out for.'

FALCONS

On one of my parents' first dates my father took my mother to a falconry show. She liked birds, she'd said when they first met. Her father's brother had been a pigeon fancier who kept his darling pigeons in a loft, and she used to help him bathe them and exercise them and ready them for competitions when she was a little girl. She would come alive when she spoke about them, and use wide, sweeping hand gestures. She had her favourite pigeons, and used to tend to their toes, soothing them with sweet almond oil and wrapping them up in cotton wool in the frost – pigeon toes are very delicate, and it's not just feral pigeons which suffer the problems that, left untreated, can lead to infection and necrosis. When she agreed to a second date my father really wanted to impress her; he had borrowed a half-decent car, and picked her up early from outside her parents' house and they drove for many hours to a place in the hills. On some of the journey she dozed and he drove, concentrating his eyes on the road, offering her water and snacks regularly.

When they arrived at the show there were lots of families in groups.

The keeper was passing the falcons around for them to be

held but my mother became anxious and refused to approach the birds.

'They aren't dangerous at all,' my father kept trying to reassure her. 'They are actually quite tame and gentle creatures.'

'Why have you brought me here?' said my mother, stepping backwards and away from the crowd.

He waited behind a family and then when it was his turn he slipped on the heavy handling glove and balanced the regal bird on his arm; it wore a brown hood with a flamboyant feather plume which was fixed under its chin. By now my mother had turned away and was standing behind a large leafy tree trying not to cry.

They left shortly afterwards. My father was dejected and confused. By all accounts it had been a disaster.

'I gather you're not a fan of those birds, then,' he had said, trying out some conversation again on the long journey back.

'What makes you think I don't like those birds?' my mother said, her face turned outwards. 'I love birds.' What she didn't tell him is that she couldn't bear to look at them in their hoods, the ones the keepers wrapped around their faces. 'Your father wasn't to know, it wasn't his fault, they keep them blind to make them quiet, you know, imagine, to keep a winged thing hostage like that, it's so horrible it makes me sick.' These words escaped from her years later when she told Rania and I the story of the falcon visit, the disaster date that made her question humanity again and vomit in a little bag on the journey back.

'I'm sorry, forgive me, it was a terrible idea,' my father apologised at the journey's end, but my mother quite unexpectedly turned towards him and smiled, and lightly touched my dad's hand. 'I know you didn't mean any harm.' It was nothing really, he was moved by this small humble gesture. He thought he was the luckiest man alive, our mother a girl who loved pigeons and blushed at the drop of a hat, which is rarer than rubies themselves. The following month my father went to the bank to check on his savings and then bought an engagement ring.

GARDENS

Not everyone has a mother who is in anxious thrall to her seedlings. My mother announced the arrival of a pond. It was going to be positioned perpendicular to what used to be the old right-hand boundary fence, chaperoned by the shade of the Indian bean tree. It would of course be filled with rainwater, its limpid surface enclosed by the brownish flowers of soft rush (*Juncus effusus*) or loosestrife (*Lysimachia vulgaris*). It would attract colonies of caddis flies, dragonflies and damselflies (their more delicate sisters). My mother was in her element, but garden ponds are supposed to require very little maintenance when they have achieved their natural balance. How do you know when they have reached their natural balance? This is the gardener's dilemma.

MEAT

'That's the last time I am eating it,' my mother says. She is standing by the cooker. 'The lamb . . . the meat . . . the sinew . . . the meat.'

'What will you eat instead?' asks Rania, flexing a finger to pinch a small parcel of lamb from the plate and sucking hard at the marrow till it capitulates and whistles. 'You can't eat air.'

'I can eat plenty.' My mother twirls (this is a special day; she twirls only in her most ecstatic moments). 'I will eat pulses. I will eat aubergines . . . '

'Stop. You're setting a bad example to your daughters,' my father interrupts.

Rania tilts her face, licking her hand right down to the knuckle.

'No shit, Sherlock,' says Rania, looking at me and winking, the juice running off the skin of her chin.

DEAR CLARE

Two days after I turned twelve my pen pal Clare told me we could no longer be friends.

> *Dear Ruby, I am really <u>sad</u> and sorry, but my dad has said I have to send you this letter and tell you I'm not allowed to be your pen friend anymore because he found out you're a Paki. I am feeling <u>sad</u> that you might be <u>sad</u> about this – I am so <u>sad</u> and sorry that we can't be friends anymore. From Clare.*

There were no kisses. She had carefully underlined the 'sad's using a ruler, but there was no pink-lined paper with cutesy animals crowded into the corner, and the perfunctory white envelope which was the repository for this four-line note contained no stickers, tattoos or glitter, and just like that my two-month correspondence with Clare Marjorie Stokely, from Diss, Norfolk, ended.

I still have the letter. I have never told anyone about its contents. I had thought of tearing it up into a hundred pieces and stuffing them in the big black bin outside the house, I had contemplated burning it on the gas stove in the kitchen. I had even thought about eating it. In the end I kept it hidden in the pocket of my *The Hunchback of Notre Dame* pop-up book, which was so large it had to lie on my bookshelf horizontally.

PLAYGROUNDS

At school I noticed that there are a lot of ways to be invisible. For example, there was Suzy, both needy and furious, who was slowly and meticulously reducing herself down, a millimetre at a time, a morsel of food less each day, whittling herself away till her shadow broke off and she disappeared. Then there was Farah. On the first day of secondary school she was the only one who didn't even have a pencil case, which matters when you're eleven – she had a plastic carrier bag, and not even a good one at that, not the type my mother might have creased out and folded away for safekeeping to produce miraculously if the need arose. Farah had a scrunched-up, unloved piece of crappy plastic for all her worldly goods.

Farah is superfluously sad; Farah doesn't say much; Farah is poor and lives with her sister, and her mother is an alcoholic who once circled the playground in a soiled dressing gown looking for her daughters. The class all watched. They pressed their noses to the glass to watch this slight, inchoate figure inching her way around the netball court lines. Farah didn't move; she stayed still, a tree at her desk, staring at her poor little hands and saying nothing. At the time I did wonder about sending Farah a note or something, but I couldn't quite reach the words I needed, and then of course the correct window of opportunity passed.

Farah and I have known each other a long time – since nursery school. So, we have history. It's not something I think she particularly dwells on nostalgically like I do. She has other priorities in her life, like making sure she and her sister are safe and getting enough to eat, and the current whereabouts of her mother. She is someone I might still talk to, though it has to be said that Farah is not great with words either, though she was a chatty little thing when she was younger. There's a photograph of us taken on the playing fields in infant school – she has her arm protectively around my shoulders and she is smiling so you can see her little beaded milk teeth. Farah smiling. This was when her parents were still together, and her mother wasn't sick or drinking or drifting aimlessly into playgrounds.

Some of the girls in the class did try with her. Occasionally one of the girls in the year would adopt her like a little pet. The girls' project was to transform Farah; they brought their makeup and clothes and lots of girly enthusiasm to the project. Farah was allowed to wear their clothes, their eyeliner, and at least it gave her a mask she could use to hide her mother-damage. Farah passively consented to this, but during the lunch hour the painted and perkier version of Farah never really looked as if her heart was in it.

I always knew how things would end. The project was always abandoned; the girls got bored or disturbed or plain just ran out of ideas.

Eventually Farah's sadness seeped out of her pores, dampened and ruined her makeup, but it didn't end there – the other girls carried her scent home, and it pervaded their own bathrooms and bedrooms till one by one they had to drop her. Farah went back to her normal clothes and her pain-stricken face and the class forgot about Farah all over again.

MAGGOTS

We learned in biology that now they can use maggots in hospitals to debride a wound in two days. The physician seals them into the infected lesion, leaves them be, and later checks the site. The skill of the procedure is this: to ensure the maggots do not overstay their welcome but reside just long enough to eat up the infected tissue before they achieve adulthood.

'I would find this unbearable,' says Farah, suddenly standing up from her stool. 'I would rather die than have someone tape flies' eggs into my skin.'

Once she said it, the air in the room seemed to change, the teacher nodded sympathetically and not one single person moved. All of us must have held the same harrowing image in our minds: plump, well-fed flies buzzing violently under gauze.

Now and then a severe-looking aunt took over when Farah's mother went absent. She collected Farah and her sister from school, fed them, and scrubbed them and their habitat scrupulously. This aunt was the exact opposite of her wayward sister. She looked exceptionally clean, had a shiny forehead and a tight bun, and wore a mackintosh buttoned up to her throat.

When it was all too much at school and she cried (which was not often), Farah cried with her non-human voice, like a helpless kitten. It's not a noise that I want to hear again.

ART

You would know a Rania painting, crowded as it is with primordial objects such as rocks, bones and mountains. My eyeballs ache when I look too long at Rania's paintings. I told Rania this one time, after she locked me in a room with them and then re-entered suddenly. She told me to close my eyes really tight then open them again and write down the first thing that came into my head. 'You mustn't think long about it, the *first* thing that comes in.' 'I feel sick, my eyeballs ache' is what I scribbled down. She seemed very satisfied and stroked my cheek and it was lovely. 'That's so good,' she said, 'because that means it's truly art.' She doesn't care for faces or people. A few years ago, Rania was doing a project and upset a lot of teachers by putting tails on all the humans in her paintings. Male and female, young and old, none were immune to the long, hairy, muscular appendage she added to her figures. My father was called in. He put on his reading spectacles and peered at his daughter's peculiar work.

'Do you see now?' insisted the head of art, huffing and puffing her way past the pottery wheels towards him. 'There's no doubt about her talent, but can't you see that what Rania has done is an abomination?' That was a hard word that stung my father.

By then Rania had had enough and decreed that if she wasn't allowed to draw the world how she saw it then she wasn't interested in drawing figures at all. From there on she refused people, animals and faces. Even hands were out of the question. In art class a cover teacher suggested she consider painting portraits – Rania put down her tools and made to leave and had to be talked down by the deputy head.

In her previous surreal phase Rania had drawn a series of paintings entitled 'From Mouth to Mouth', consisting of people inside gigantic mouths open wide. A little girl (which I presume was a version of the artist) stood on the tongue floor, and above her, from the mouth's palate, the uvula hung down like some awful pink church bell.

She even managed to sell two of these paintings going door to door. I accompanied her to Camden, holding her canvases and loitering near the gates of the tall houses. At one house a couple ushered us both into their huge living room, in the corner of which were different-sized pairs of green wellington boots; each pair seemingly had its own personality. We sat on the tiredest and longest leather sofa in the world and the whole room smelt of feet and books and it was nice.

Rania introduced me as her artist's assistant.

'She's really quiet and spiritual and thinks deeply about the artistic process,' she explained to the middle-aged couple, and they nodded in a sympathetic way, and then chatted to Rania whilst I extracted a pear from deep inside my jacket pocket and ate it, stalk and pips included. The woman brought over a dusty wine bottle. 'This is how you can tell if it's a good bottle of wine,' she winked. Rania looked at me and smiled politely, waiting for the revelation. 'Here,' the woman said and took Rania's hand and placed it at the bottom of the shapely bottle. 'Feel that dip? How deep that well is? That's how you know. The deeper the well, the finer the wine.' The three of them laughed like cousins and whilst they poured and drank, I left the room in search of a bathroom. A large washroom was located on the half landing; it had a treasure trove on a narrow console display table, including items such as a shiny little antique pistol with a mother-of-pearl handle (very worn) and a Victorian jar full of pink and blue cotton-wool boules. I held the pistol and put the tip of the barrel in my mouth and tried to slip my tongue into the hole. It tasted of old incense. I pushed the pistol in my pocket to replace the pear, but it felt wrong to replace the dignity of a warm pear with a heavy, cold, inhumane object. When I made to leave the room, however, the pistol softly squeaked like a soon-to-be-abandoned kitten and I moved towards it and regarded it again. I looked in the mirror and my eyes were shining, which was usually a good omen, and I decided to keep it and slipped it into my pocket again.

'They loved the pear thing, that was priceless,' said Rania later on the train. 'I could tell they were impressed.'

Rania came away with £200, a list of contacts and the compliment that her art was 'simultaneously visionary and compelling and flowering with tumescent wisdom'. But two doors earlier another woman said she thought the paintings were derivative, creations of crap, and so it was difficult for Rania to know what kind of mood to be in.

'Can something be brilliant and bad at the same time?' mused Rania on the way home. She was flushed with wine and her tongue was stained and smelt of an intoxicating mix of overripe blackberries and blood. That smell, I need to remember, that is what I imagine sex must smell like.

PLAYGROUNDS

In the last year of primary school Robin Osborne, a boy in my class I never noticed, gave me a small gold heart. He came to my desk in the middle of a lesson and lightly placed the thin metal object next to my pencil case then quickly returned to his seat. There were a few gasps from the class, and the teacher smiled stupidly from her desk. Clearly a response was required, but I was bewildered. For weeks I turned it over in my head. Did I love him? And what about David, who might not have hearts to give but was the first boy I kissed and his little hands were never cold. Could I love Robin? I wanted to love him, that much was true. I observed his face discreetly but closely during silent meditation in assemblies, and in our PE lessons I noticed how his fringe could puff up romantically in the wind.

Once I had finally decided I desired Robin Osborne more than anything else in the world I discovered he had moved on. He had gone over to Jacqueline-of-the-sinewy-limbs, member of the netball team, and I couldn't compete with a goal shooter – I couldn't compete with that. I was having a bout of crepitus in my knees and jumping for a ball caused both pain and humiliation. I knew it was only a matter of time before he would deliver her a gold heart at her desk. And yes, the day came when he gave Jacqueline a gold heart identical to mine, and I sat and pushed my heels down to fuse myself to the floor, and tried to work on my protective glaze face I'd practised in the mirror for these types of eventualities.

I could see now that Robin had mean and tight little features.

Maybe David wasn't so bad after all. I had ignored him for ages even though he had appeared at my doorstep with letters and made me a gift of a fish with origami scales that would have involved hours of tedious folding. I had neglected him badly. I had overlooked his virtues. He was complicated and sensitive and had been adopted. Robin was a fraud but David was the real thing. Suddenly all my happy feelings for him came flooding back. I couldn't wait to see him, my mind a small restless animal all day long. After school I followed the long familiar path to his house past the twin monkey puzzle trees and the loop in the road which led to his gate. But David and his family had moved. He never told me. No one told me he was going. The front door opened and a little girl aged about seven came out and scowled at me and then smiled. That is what it's like at that age, you are testing yourself out, how you can be cruel and amiable in the space of a moment, which is why playgrounds are such terrible places. David was flower-delicate and had a fragile soul and a lucky yellow marble he let me touch from time to time.

DAVID GIRDLESTON
EATS CRANE FLIES

I don't know if you've ever got up close to a crane fly. In their infant stage, they lie buried as leatherjackets in the soil, passive until September when they finally wake and their whimsical bodies emerge from the vegetation.

They have a fey, other-worldly quality about them, they drift rather than fly and are easily caught. At the end of October, or sometimes sooner, you'll get a cold spell that kills them off almost overnight. But in the first few weeks of autumn term our school seemed to have a ceaseless supply. They must have bred in the long grassy areas around the dozen mobile classrooms that had been erected on a temporary basis (though I was in one for four years). In winter, if your form teacher was late, you would have no choice but to stand freezing your feet off waiting for them to arrive with the keys. The mobile huts themselves had a provisional air; the hollow raised floors, the heating delivered out of two skinny electric radiators that didn't have timers, so on Monday winter mornings we sat with our frozen fingers defrosting in our coats. We knew the teachers detested the huts as much as we did, which is why they avoided coming near them at breaktimes even though they must have known about the smoking, the making out, the fights around the back of them.

In the warmer weeks in September, some of the kids would congregate near the huts at breaktimes or lunches. David stood waiting, leaning on one of the sheds, smoking a tiny cigarette. I had been both nervous and excited when I realised we were in the same senior school, but once there David had kept his distance. He smoked using his index finger and his thumb, bringing the roll-up very close to his mouth, almost kissing his finger. His friend Gary stood in the middle of the crowd collecting coins from the circle of kids around him. Kirsty, who was Gary's stepsister, was the lookout, and gave them both the nod at which David took his cue, very coolly threw down the cigarette stub and walked over. They had done some of the work, had collected a dozen or so and placed them in a Tupperware container. I don't know when they had been caught but once the lid was off it was clear many of the flies had died. David picked the dead ones out with his fingers and flicked them onto the ground.

One or two of the spectators groaned. David peered into the box and lifted one out. This one was about just alive; its puny legs kicked out pathetically, and if you got close enough to tune in you might hear it crying. The crowd went quiet and tense; he opened his mouth really wide and pushed the fly in.

Some of the kids started making vomiting noises, others were just quietly incredulous. David looked over towards Kirsty for a steer and she smiled and nodded, and he opened his mouth really wide and held out his tongue.

Kirsty offered the box again. David took one more and placed it in his mouth, and this time he made this big thing of chewing it and swallowing it slowly and deliberately and then he took another, followed by four or five more, and smiled theatrically and burped. The crowd erupted, but then the bell rang, and the kids started to disperse. After the show the spectators filed out quickly and silently past David, their eyes avoiding him.

David just lit another cigarette, dropping the match down at his feet whilst Gary and Kirsty counted the money, placing the coins into small stacks on the steps.

He moved over to the other side, panting lightly as he leant his body sideways against the hut, humming a tune I didn't know the words to. I didn't want him to see me, then. I wondered if he remembered anything about us. In school he passed me in corridors and rarely acknowledged me, and the other times he would nod or look embarrassed because I saw him being reprimanded for a fight or for cutting classes. Everyone had gone now, and I waited carefully just underneath the steps, feeling heavy thinking of David and his goodness slowly being ruined, all the hope draining out of me. I was late for registration but still I couldn't move, and I waited until the cold came up from the ground and into my feet. I didn't have my coat on and pretty soon I was shivering.

In the following weeks he did a few more shows around the huts. The same routine. Then he disappeared. We heard rumours; something about a spell up at St Bernard's, something about glue sniffing, but anyway by then it was the end of October and the weather had turned and annihilated the crane flies.

GARDENS

Everyone who knows even a little about gardens soon learns that the art of gardening is a futile attempt (or a sequence of futile attempts) to reconcile oppositional forces at work in the area. On the one hand you're trying to tempt beneficial birds and insects, and on the other hand you're repudiating moles and containing weeds and blight and battling with bodies of earwigs.

If you plant a tree you have to accept it will be somebody else's shade. Birds you will probably never see will discover it and make use of its branches to nest in.

FUNGI

Once my mother bought me a large lined notebook called a dream journal, with a soft cover and a pale sketch of hummingbirds in flight on each page. Most of the time I made up entries about shadowy, tall men who lay down with me in the woods on the carpet of deadly fungi and we were as naked as roosters.

CONTRACT

'Ruby, will you sign the holy contract?'

I signed the paper in my best-ever handwriting. I knew what a signature was, and its importance. I had two notebooks chock-full of my potential signatures. But this was the first time I would use one for a real-life contract, plus I had witnesses, so I applied my name carefully and slowed down so everyone would notice it, especially the little flourishes at the end. Everyone who attended Mrs Kendrick's Thursday lunchtime Bible classes had to sign the contract. Mrs Kendrick's two monitors were tasked with recruitment and the important administrative role of checking the contract and ensuring compliance. I had signed the contract, and in a short time Jesus was going to save me. This was going to be very exciting, not because I believed it but because if I failed to turn up, I would be in breach of my contract and there would be consequences. Though I couldn't imagine what they might be, they sounded transgressive and alluring. I knew that if you failed to attend then the monitors would be sent into the playground to smoke you out, and you couldn't hide in the back of the toilets because that was the very first place they would look. It was clear why they had recruited me; I was an easy target. The non-talking frequently need saving.

Mrs Kendrick picked up a guitar from her folk-bag and started singing hosannas. We had built up to it, she warmed us up first with the Lord's Prayer followed by a little Jesus fable from one of her picture books, usually with a stupid lamb being rescued by a good Samaritan, out of the death-jaws of a violent river or a steep ravine where the brainless creature had somehow got trapped. Next she would lick her lips and slip into a dreamlike reverie, her voice high and shrill, her glossy, honey-coloured guitar swaying, the whites of her eyes upwards towards the holiness.

'Join in, join in, children,' she would half scream as the monitors shook the tambourines and juggled the Spanish maracas importantly and we sang till Jesus heard us. Afterwards Mrs Kendrick looked frazzled, as if she'd just come out of a spin dryer, because the spirit had drained every ounce of life from her, and then her exertions were over; her dark-shouldered sleeves were showered with dandruff and finally the biscuits from the special octagonal tin were distributed throughout the classroom.

Pretty soon I got bored of Mrs Kendrick's Thursday lunch-times. I looked around at all the faces in the final prayers of all the children praying hard for grandparents and parents to get better or to come home, to stop drinking wine, for pets to be better or last a little longer. I looked at the monitors who everyone resented because they had all the powers of the contract and saw that they were praying blindly for something banal, and it all felt so hoaxy and selfish. I went home that very night and looked on my father's desk for words in his office papers that might help me: *hereby*, *whereas*, *notwithstanding*, none of it made any sense at first, but after I had made it up and read it a few times my letter made more sense than their original contract had.

I would not give it to the monitors, I needed to give it to the source. The next day I waited outside the staffroom and knocked; a coffee-breathed young teacher I didn't know came to the door, and I passed him the letter for Mrs Kendrick.

'Wait a minute,' he said and then Mrs Kendrick herself appeared at the door and opened and read the letter right in front of me. 'What a horrible cold little thing you are,' she said and then let one of the teachers pass, retracting her claws for a moment and flashing him a rictus smile.

'Well, that's extremely disappointing, Ruby, and the devil works in mysterious ways.' She checked her temper, I noticed her hands were trembling slightly. She continued, 'I would never have expected this from you, a girl like you; I singled you out especially and I think you've let yourself down.' *And and and . . .* she went on. I retrieved the letter from her hands, smiled and left before she could finish her sentence.

SPEECH

Here are a few things I have to say on the subject of human utterance:

1. Everything worth saying can be written on your fingernail or on the seam of an unshelled almond.
2. The first thing you start doing when you start talking is editing.
3. Look in the margins for the truth.
4. This is more a commitment than a theory, like the tadpole's commitment to the pond, always its eyes, always its ears.

They say you need to have clocked up more than ten thousand hours to excel in any skill. Not many young adults are experts at anything, but I think I am an expert in the art of solitude and quietness. It's something I've worked hard at and practised and studied like a Venetian master glass-blower who can puff up a little bit of white-hot jelly-glass and transform it into a fruit bowl or a horse rearing up in battle.

I lead my teachers and my peers to endless head-scratching, because silence and shyness are to be overcome, battled and grappled with; choosing not to talk when you are able is just ungrateful. At junior school it was a little easier simply being known as the dumb dumb-girl, where I discovered burning dimly has its advantages.

Now I am continually being pressed on the subject of my quietude. My quiet-as-a-mouse status is strangely disruptive, particularly when it's accompanied by my school reports. Because my IQ is too high, my exam results are too good, and yet still I choose against speech – my teachers' empathic nerves flicker less when they try to get their heads around this.

This was at the time that I realised that if I closed my eyes I could disappear into myself and walk straight through the walls, or into the carpet, through the floorboards, through the cracks in the brickwork, the mortar, to the garden, and into the soil right through to the resting shiny body of a worm.

Absenting yourself is not the antidote to sadness, says one therapist. *There's safety in language. When are you going to realise all the harm you could do by not using your voice?* says another. I dutifully take down these wisdoms in my most shapely script in my notebook.

And what about all the bad men? says Rania. *What about that doctor who came to St Mary's School and made the girls lie down and he looked into their mouths with a tiny torch and he made them say 'ah, ah' when all the while pressing on their breasts or their crotches.* I am surprised that she recalls this as only a few of the girls complained and those that used their voices were ignored and the only way the bad doc got caught was because one girl bit him hard enough to draw blood, using her central incisors.

When I moved to my new school my father took me to one side.

'This is an opportunity to be normal, Ruby. No one knows you — you can try out a new persona, new start. Will you try, Ruby?'

I nodded in all seriousness. I could try out the other Ruby, it could be like wearing somebody else's coat.

PLAYGROUNDS

'What's the matter with you, girl?' the history teacher had asked me for the third time, and then I was beginning to itch all over. I don't remember much, only a sound that began like a whine in my middle ear and spread thickly through me till it finished in my stomach. All this must have happened very quickly as my body flopped to the floor to the sound of a thousand pins dropping all around me.

Now the teachers don't push me in my classes. Occasionally they will read out a piece of my writing, like the final paragraph of my essay on *Orlando*. We had just been studying *An Inspector Calls* but I thought it was preachy and unoriginal and told me nothing new. '*Orlando*, in all its shape-shifting and surging dreams, and with all its angular beauty, was a book which I felt deeply and strangely connected to. Was Orlando a girl? Was Orlando a boy? Does Orlando have a penis or a uterus or maybe both?' The teacher had given me an A but also written in the margin: 'Parts of this essay are bizarre and suffused with an unhealthy obsession with the sublime!'

Therapist Number Four had induced me to draw shapes and respond to her questions quickly with one-line notes, like last lines of poems. Once or twice I dropped in something slant like a line by Emily Dickinson to see if she noticed. Next week I might try Bowie.

'Who can you imagine being friends with?' says this therapist. I gaze down at my notebook a bit too long for her liking.

'It's not a trick question. You don't need to be clever about it. I need you to respond as quickly and naturally as possible.'

I chew my pencil a little bit more.

'It's just a provocation.' She tempted me out.

Sometimes I hate you, I wrote finally and turned the notebook around.

She blinked rapidly whilst she read it. 'Well that's the most unguarded you've been. Well done, it was pure and honest, and you shouldn't feel bad about writing it as it reveals something about you.' I felt happy to have gifted her this.

I had obviously aroused something in her, and she started scribbling in her file, her engagement ring flashing. And I could see the seeds of respect growing in her for the first time ever.

SCHEHERAZADE

As everyone knows, Scheherazade was a talker. In an age when there was a real shortage of female talkers, in an age when seasoned liars were punished by having their tongues removed and fed to the king's cats, this woman talked. This particular king was the same man who had murdered hundreds of fresh, anonymous virgins, brought to his rooms night after night. Do you know their names? No, neither do I. I think of them sometimes being delivered through the gates of the palace, trembling in their perfumed carriages, their small delicate feet on the royal bed linen, their long, dark hair spread out on the bolsters. Were they voiceless? Did they go unwillingly? Were they drugged up or lied to, did they struggle? Did he bait them or flip them over before he violently deflowered them? Then he had their necks sliced by the sword of his courtier, before they stepped, blinking, into his bougainvillea-filled courtyard in the first light of the new morning. Scheherazade neutralised the threat. Scheherazade is 'world-freer' in Arabic. But who exactly did she free? All the sources say the villages were running out of girls. And still there was The Monster, a mass murderer; she had his children and stayed married to him for the rest of her life.

PLAYGROUNDS

It's safe to say that Rania was the difficult daughter. Rania was the spirited, disruptive one. She was the daughter who tried to bring foxes into the house, the one who tried to operate on her friends with sterilised safety pins, and the one who lured me into the old chest freezer in the shed, that one you could only open from the outside. Somehow my skin-of-her-teeth sister was allowed to remain in school. She was the one who retaliated when Mr Bagley, the geography teacher, threw a bullet of chalk at her. It bounced off her forehead. She stood up and blurted out, 'Wanker.' Mr Bagley's face reddened.

'What did you say?'

Rania rubbed her forehead but stood her ground. She was escorted to the head's office, where Mrs Cumberland, who was on the cusp of retirement, swished around nervously in her black robes.

'Wanker. *Wanker*,' repeated Mr Bagley; he kept repeating the word because he actually really liked saying it, the hardness of the word, and the look on the head teacher's face – her flinch-and-rest every time he pushed out the word. No one investigated why Mr Bagley was allowed to hurl hard pieces of chalk at his pupils, and neither did they investigate why he was inviting sixth-form girls over to his flat at weekends to play his white-reggae records. Rania was never suspended for that incident, or for smoking and fighting, or for getting mixed up with boys. She was finally suspended after she threw a tampon across the classroom for a dare and it landed in Alison Riley's spirally hair and hung there limply like a stunned bird, after which Mrs McGee needed a sedative from the staffroom medical cupboard and also something for her bunionettes.

NEEDLES

Farah visits. She has brought a list of food items she will not eat. She has to bring along her younger sister and asks if that's OK. Her sister is now called MJ; that was definitely not what she was called a few months ago but maybe she's trying her on for size, auditioning this MJ character, and the original Nina is waiting in the wings until her services are required.

We walk home the long way through the park. MJ is chattier than Farah and Nina, more confident, and she confides in me; she's going to work for an Arab airline so she can wear a little red hat with a side veil and marry a sheikh or a pilot or a salesman with beautiful teeth. She runs all over the place and hides behind the bushes and tries to make us laugh. She does cartwheels and doesn't seem to care that everyone can see the white knickers under her skirt. Farah looks disgusted by her sister, and so I perform the big sister's task of holding MJ's coat and bag and waiting for her whilst she climbs a tree. I hold the tree like you would a ladder, and look out for her safety as her real sister continues to ignore her.

'She is trying to impress you,' says Farah, finally, looking down at her poor feet. 'She's trying to make you like her more than me.'

That's the thing with Farah: she'll be really quiet and then will say something devastating like that, not a polite conversation-opener like most normal people, but something dark and psychologically dramatic and disturbing that shuts you down, talker or no talker. I give her nothing but I pat her on her shoulder a few times, and hope she understands I am still her friend and could never prefer any version of her sister to her – definitely not this masquerading sister with all the moves and the swagger; and not the original, forgettable Nina either.

There was a time that Farah had birthday parties, and we brought her wrapped presents like pencil cases and a pink hairdryer, and she had a special iced birthday cake in the shape of a peacock, and her special friends were allowed to stay and use the paddling pool.

Farah's sister climbs down from the tree and grabs her things from my arms.

My sister meets us on the way home, and two older boys come along and walk beside us and start talking. Rania is always being approached by men. One of the younger guys has a dog on a lead.

'Don't smile or talk to those boys. It only encourages them and then we'll have to listen to all their crap,' says my sister to us in a wise fashion. Rania is dressed in cropped jeans and a slouchy cardigan that shows off a triangle of her brown shoulder, and she's tied up her hair really high, so it looks like she's balancing a big black ball on her head. Farah stops to stroke the dog and something about that image startles me: Farah displaying such kindness and the dog liking her back. For a moment it's nice, two pairs of sisters walking down a road, all heading the same way, Farah forgetting herself and stroking the dog. Me the outie sister with my cool innie sister, with her slopy angles and her poufy hair.

The boy asks MJ if she and Farah are sisters and she says, 'No,' quickly flashing her little teeth, and the swiftness of the denial, so emphatic and reflexive, makes me wince. I look over at Farah, but she doesn't look at me and I decide that I preferred old Nina, who may have been quieter and less fun but whose animal was probably a gazelle, whereas MJ deserves to be a mean animal like a hawk or a rattlesnake.

Just then Rania swoops down to the pavement to attend to a stricken bee.

'Till my mortal breath I will save that bee,' she laughs, trying to move the blurry creature out of harm's way with the edge of a credit card. The face of one of the boys suddenly softens, and he crouches down beside her and then they are both laughing, and before you know it, they are exchanging phone numbers and addresses and talking about concerts at Wembley.

I take her hand as we cross the road and then I take Farah's hand too.

We eat dinner together later at our house. Rania always loves cooking; she likes to experiment with robust flavours, always adding too much garlic or chilli or onion.

This time she's made some rich and strange sauce; it's over-salted and hot and delicious and Farah stirs the pasta around and around on her plate. MJ reaches over to take her sister's leftovers. My sister seems to think she's hilarious, this new-edition sister of Farah, and soon they are both standing next to the sink messing around with the washing-up and squirting each other with bubbles like some terrible yet perfectly improvised advertisement for sisterliness. Both Farah and I remain at the table looking at each other, and then she looks down – either she's looking at her hands or at the woven table mat.

Rania tries to persuade MJ that she should have a nose piercing.

Rania had pierced herself all over, but nothing gave her greater pleasure than inserting holes in other people's skin and cartilage, and she did it for free.

'I could do your nose! You have the kind of nose that could take a piercing – not everyone's nose can, but I can see it really working on you.'

'Really? Do you think so?' MJ wrinkles her nose. 'Why don't you have one in your nose?'

'I did, but I took it out, as I don't think my nose can carry it, and I have loads everywhere else. Shall I get the needles?'

'I'm not sure; I don't like needles.'

'Oh, don't worry about that. I use a special needle – no one ever feels it.'

'I'll do it,' says Farah, looking up and facing Rania. 'I will do it right now.'

Rania looks at Farah and made a calculation in her head.

'I'm not sure,' says Rania, looking genuinely wary.

'You were going to do it to my younger sister, but you won't do it for me?' says Farah.

'Let's both do it!' says MJ.

'Shut the fuck up,' says Farah, louder than I have ever heard her speak, and Rania looks from one sister to the other, her curiosity piqued by the strange little sisterly psychodrama playing out at the kitchen table.

'I'll get the ice,' says Rania. She quickly returns with ice, antiseptic spray, her surgical gloves and paper towels, upon which she arranges her assortment of needles and studs.

I watch the little procedure as Rania measures, then angles the needle and jabs the long steel tube into Farah's nose and out through her nostril, before quickly feeding the stud through to its resting place. I can hear Farah breathing rapidly, but no tears, no blood, no screaming.

Rania has been making reassuring nursey noises like, 'Good girl, you're doing great,' throughout the procedure, and looks thrilled with the result and passes Farah the mirror. 'It looks amazing on you.'

'Thanks,' says Farah, barely glancing at it.

After dinner Farah is lying on my bed with her hands underneath her head, her sharp elbows pointed up into the air. I am sitting cross-legged by her side, but I am so close to her face that I can see the pale blue puff-cushions under her eyes like little parcels of pain. I have this urge to press my thumbs gently on each one to see if anything flows out. The stud in her nose is glinting like a star. I am sitting so close to her that I won't have to go beyond a whisper. I can overhear her heart muscles contracting. She is wearing one of Rania's oversized grey jumpers, which makes her look smaller and paler than she is. She rereads the little story I've written about a leopard mother losing her cub to a python. The leopard hunts down the killer python and in a wild panic the snake regurgitates the remains of her baby leopard. Mother stands over the decaying flesh-remains of her cub for a long time, as if she was praying over her baby's corpse, then with great care and attention mummy leopard eats every particle of her cub and then returns home to grieve under the dappled shade of a tree for several days without eating again all that time. I watched it on a documentary but in my story the animals all have names and voices and it's a sort of fable.

'Why are your stories so sad?' Farah waves the pages over her face and balances them in her hands. Farah has such beautiful hands. Someone should paint her hands; they are creaturely and move with bird-grace. I want to tell Farah that I thought the story was beautiful; the python does what is expected of the python, but the mummy leopard eating every part of her baby is an act of love. I am not sure how much more I could explain this even if I could utter it. Everyone thinks leopards should sound like cats, but their sound resembles a bark.

Sometimes Farah asks me for a sound and on occasion I give her one. Vowels are hard; you might think they are easier, but the problem with vowels is not knowing their ultimate destination. Plus, there are the vibrations, which feel like something, like a disturbance or a fly trapped in your brain. At least with a 'k' or a 'p' or 'd' they are containable and measurable. Once a vowel is in your mouth you have to submit to it fully. I move carefully towards her and lay myself down on her still body and she strokes my hair and we stay like this for a long time. I couldn't conceive of anything better in the universe than lying on her lovely body like this her heart fluttering underneath mine our fingers threaded together, our breath as fast as kittens'.

THE PARTY

That same night I have a dream that I am standing in a corner by myself at a party, naked except for a piano shawl decorating my shoulders.

In the morning Rania announces that I have to accompany her to an actual party. I am not one for parties. Rania needed me to accompany her so badly she invited Farah as well. Rania really wants to go, and she has thought carefully about the game plan with my father. When she is arguing her case, her talking is speeded up, she's a bit breathy with trying to dampen down any particle of desire or excitement in her body that my father might detect, unearth and quell.

We get a little lost trying to find the house, Rania is looking nervous, and before we approach the security gates, she presses hard on my arm till I almost squeak. 'Don't let me down, girls,' she keeps saying. 'Just for fuck's sake try to be normal.' Farah smiles wryly.

So, the three of us arrive at this party. Rania has on a white dress which hugs her hips and dangerous shiny little shoulders, and she's put me in one of her funky T-shirt dresses with a black choker and some smoky eye makeup. I rub out and reapply the sticky mocha lip gloss till my lips are sore and take on a life of their own; on the tube I fiddle with the choker till

Rania scowls at me. Farah is wearing a fawn-coloured dress with big hooped earrings, her hair all washed and fragrant.

The party is in a huge house in the posh part of town. A maid answers the door and without a second look Rania immediately heads over to a crowd of people she knows; on the train she sweetly told me to have a nice time and that no one gives a fuck about how much I'll be talking – in fact it's probably an asset – and that all they will care about is having some exotic young Indian girls at the party. The hall is not like a normal hall, more like a long, unfurnished room, and there is an oversized dramatic painting taking up the space on one wall; it's all lit up from above with a tiny row of picture lamps and if you step back you can see in the foreground three small figures – tall black lean men leaning on canes in somewhere like Kenya. A couple of guests are looking at it, bending and arching their bodies to get a fresh look from a distance.

'It's extraordinary – I mean it's so moving in its simplicity,' says the woman.

'Yes, I agree,' says the man. 'It's powered by its artlessness.'

Farah and I stand at the edges of the main room like over-age orphans. There's a man in a really cool suit, with tapered trousers which finish short on his leg; he's sweating gently in his expensive jacket. Then there's a group of loud men with girlfriends who won't leave their sides. In our corner this is the choice: a young, enthusiastic man with two moles either side of his face (one of which resembles a worm cast); or a man with a nice square face under a thick, uncontrollable mop of black hair, with hairy wrists and hands, and fingers and knuckles to accompany them. They have names like Russell or Dominic.

A Russell/Dominic leans forward to talk and Farah is all of a sudden perky, upright and annoyingly attentive. Russell/Dominic has a watch, the face of which looks old and expensive, with a thin bezel of gold and a leather strap which looks new. I must have been staring at the watch, because Russell/Dominic removes his important timepiece and gives it to me to hold.

'It's kind of an heirloom,' he says. I turn the watch over, and lo and behold on the back is an old inscription etched into the metal, almost faded. I am holding in my hands the oldest item I have ever held, and I wonder if that makes it a significant day. Russell/Dominic has round light brown eyes, a bit like the gentle bear's I stared into once at the zoo.

'You're very beautiful. You have beautiful skin.' He says this after smiling at me through his glass whilst he takes a sip of orange whisky.

'Thanks,' I mouth very carefully, and I feel the choker tightening around my throat, beginning to strangle me. I've realised that parties like this are a great place to contort my mouth into various positions, where it might appear to people that I am talking and emitting words and sentences when in fact no trace of a sound comes out.

I can tell Russell/Dominic really needs or wants to dance. His feet are tapping furiously.

'My parents were very Methodist – very strict – no television, no papers or dancing because, what do they say, the devil has all the best tunes?'

He thinks he's really funny and Farah is laughing loudly. I take a look at his thick wrists. He was no Methodist. I didn't believe a word of it. He did not appear to have melancholic bones.

Sometimes I do this: I imagine being stark naked in the sheets of a bed with a man. I close my eyes and let my mind follow through like a film; it's a good way of auditioning a prospective man that I may one day cross that threshold with. And then sometimes later, when I am underneath my own bedcovers, I might try with my own two bony fingers or a malleable pillow. I go into this space with Russell/Dominic. I lift up my arm and comb a hand though his hair, but the hair is deep like unkempt grass and my entire hand goes in and pushes and I still haven't reached the bottom, and then I am elbow-deep in the dirty hair of a man, I am still not even touching the roots, and then I begin to panic and quickly rescue my hand.

Rania once went into an artist's graphic detail about what one looks like, which confirmed a lot of what I had guessed anyway, and to be honest I'll be more than content if I never see one as long as I live. She's told me stories of dating men who are boring and say things like: 'You've got to be in it to win it,' or 'There's more than one way of skinning a cat,' and how she has to pinch herself awake all evening; there were other men whose fingers (as thick as Cuban cigars) tried to find her crotch underneath the tablecloth in restaurants. I had already decided that when I was older, I was going to carry a little knife in a leather sheath in my boots or shoes. Apparently, some Taiwanese women order the knives small enough to slide them into their vagina. I remember the stolen Victorian gun and a little erotic charge seizes my body. I check my little bag for the teeny pistol; I've folded a pad of tissues to cushion it and it's reassuring just looking at it curled up asleep like that. I decide I like carrying a gun.

The room is so crowded. Hairy man and nice-faced man are leaning in and talking at us, and I can't hear anything it's so noisy, and I blur my eyes so all the people in the room turn to a mass of indistinct shadows. That was the only way I had been able to make sense of it all at school; all the beating bodies herded together in the assembly room or all those flapping limbs in the playing fields. I think this is the reason I find rainstorms so satisfying, that afterwards it will end in the rainblur on the windows, and the drops rattling on and on, pelting the bowls outside, and you can close your eyes till something gives way to contentment.

Rania is now on the other side of the room (she really did mean it when she said that she was going to ignore us all evening) gliding on her thin heels, holding a thin glass of something pale and bubbly and lightly laughing. Now and then a man will hold her waist and then she'll move a little way away, then another man will circle her waist, or she'll laugh, but judge it very carefully so that she laughs with her whole body at a slinky angle, her long neck taut and vulnerable, her hip bent just so. Farah is drinking too, but she manages to do this sadly, like she's at a dentist's waiting for a root canal extraction without anaesthetic. I wish I could touch a switch and be back in my bed next to the radiator, with my purple duvet.

I wish for things to be simple, you could take two little pink pills like you can to support your digestive system after mealtimes, or maybe recite a mantra as an antidote for dis-illusionment and apathy, or a spell to prevent the beautiful giraffes slipping from the endangered list to the critical list. Before I've thought any more deep thoughts Farah is knocking back whatever comes around to us, and the phrase *the apple doesn't fall far from the tree* floats into my mind, and then immediately I hate myself for thinking such a mean, stupid thing about my best friend who I've dragged to this fucking party. The slip of used-up lemon on the table eyeballs me, and I wonder if those seeds of pity are actually for myself, and I wonder if I should have a drink after all.

By one a.m. Farah and I are both on the dance floor in the garden, her bare arms soft wings around me. There are bodies scattered all over the garden by now, watermelon rinds are squiggling like poisonous snakes in the grass, waiters have started scraping the cream and the expensive cheese glued to the plates off into the bin, and there are couples in deep and fascinating conversations about the cosmos. Farah and I are still rocking around in each other's arms. I am scared to stop moving because if I stop everything keeps going on without me, and I don't want to start vomiting because I hate to puke more than anything else in the world. Now and then Farah stops and makes me open my mouth to spill in some full fat Cola.

I love you, I tell her, and I'm not sure if I uttered the words into the air or if I said them in my head, but she's laughing and calling me silly and she kisses me on the forehead and then I pass out.

It must be very early in the morning, because in the corner of the conservatory a serious, sober, expensive woman is diligently applying makeup, getting ready to go to work.

I hear laughter, and there is Farah expertly smoking a cig-arette, her legs crossed at the ankles. She's sipping elegantly from a big cup as she is chatting at the table, someone called Antonia says her name and I feel a pinch of jealousy – she looks normal and beautiful, or she's done a really good job of acting that way, which is equally impressive. It makes me feel strange seeing her like this, like the door to Farah's secret interior has suddenly been flipped open. It would have been less odd to wake up and see her scaling the vast roof of the house and abseiling down to the patio.

She sees I'm awake and comes over with the mug.

'Your sister's still upstairs with that Toby guy. Here,' she says, 'drink this – there's lots of sugar in it.' I nod my head gratefully and drink.

On the train on the way home I feign nausea and fatigue; I can't bear to look at this Farah who is being so very attentive, the Farah who passes me face wipes and who urges me to drink water. How well can you know anybody, really?

When we get to the station, she leans forward to try to hug me and I put my hand in the way.

'Bye then,' she says. She waits for me to reply. I shrug my shoulders. 'Ruby. I haven't changed. I just want to try to be normal. I was supposed to have a different life before my father died. I was supposed to have a life with enough money and a normal mum and all that and I am sure you want to be normal too.'

Normal. I looked down. She said the word *died* in a peculiar way as if she finished the sentence with a question. She used both words like they were big discoveries, like a new door she's come across in a corridor. But the doors have always been there, and in the past, she's been content to ignore them, or else resent their pockmarks, and now she wants to try to push them all open.

'Are you listening?' Farah persists. 'Because sometimes I think you are drifting further and further from what is normal.' I meet Farah's eyes. Somehow, she has managed to remove nearly every trace of last night's makeup, and her cheeks have a pearly glow. Normalhood really suits her.

'Give me something, Ruby,' Farah tries. 'We are still mates, right? Say something. Say something back.' My mouth is very dry. Tears are filling her eyes. I look at Farah. I mean really look at her and drink her in. I don't know what it is at that moment, but her familiar scent has just evaporated. Then finally the wind tosses up her lovely hair and I know it's over.

The next time I see her at school she's been adopted by her classmates again and is becoming prettified. This time the makeup sticks and the clothes hang spectacularly on her long body. She is spectacular. Her little teeth are glinting in happiness. When I am in the library, I meet her in the doorway; her eye makeup is in three different shades and matches her jumper, good for her. This is Farah. The other Farah is dying softly in another room.

DE-CATASTROPHISATION
(FOR BEGINNERS)

Mrs Boland likes to offer me lifts into school. Mrs Boland is the careers teacher.

From the corner of my vision I can see she has stopped the car and put on her hazard lights. I keep my head down and my hood up, but she gets out of the car and is standing, waving.

'Hop in, Ruby – it will save you from the rain!' she shouts. It's not raining yet, but the clouds look a bit threatening.

'I heard your mother's gone away again?' she begins. Mrs Boland always likes to enquire about my mother. 'It's OK to be sad about your mother; it must be terribly hard on you and your sister . . . '

Mrs Boland is the sort of person I should like on paper, but I don't as a real, warm-blooded human being. Mainly because she's so noisy, but also because I can detect a volatile temperament. Anyway, I accept my fate: ten minutes' exposure to this woman who has a strange method of driving, rarely using her mirrors and preferring to swing her body around violently to check for cars when overtaking. She's wearing dainty, soft tan gloves with punched-out shapes around the edges. I look about me and I have a sudden desire to raid her glove compartment, but instead I recklessly wind down the window one and a half inches. Mrs Boland is Canadian and met and fell in love with Mr Boland, the head of science, when she was here on a gap year many decades ago. Mr and Mrs Boland are known to be strong traditional Buddhists (which Mrs Boland pronounces *Boodist*, as in *Boo*, said the ghost.)

Some people say Mrs Boland's husband was suspended as head of science after he was spotted shouting 'power to the people' on a picket line outside Hounslow bus station whilst wearing a donkey jacket. Other people say he was put on sick leave after he asked a group of girls to smell his fingers after a science experiment.

'It's OK not to want to talk,' continues Mrs Boland. 'Heaven knows it's a normal reaction to what you've been through — our minds are very strong, it's understandable, perfectly natural . . . ' and she went on understanding, empathising with my poor, thin, blighted mother and praising my sister's spirited disposition and her mordant wit, and then finally praising my tongueless brilliance.

Mrs Boland has a compulsion to ornament her talking. Her words come fast and impassioned and her speech is flecked with interjections.

'Listen, Ruby, look, you're a bright girl and you should go to university. Wow. University, how to explain? University is where you might be able to find yourself, your voice, hey? Your people.'

Mrs Boland is someone who should occasionally partake in the quality of speechlessness. Mrs Boland gives everything away even if you don't want it. I don't need to see her living room and bedrooms; I already know there will be womb-red bedspreads with chinoiserie, and framed miniature prints from the Kama Sutra in the bathroom. We drive into the staff car park and I have to walk past the head of biology, Dr Sharma, but because I am with Mrs Boland this immunises me from his usual look of pity or scorn or rage, which is exchanged for one of curiosity and intrigue.

'So, I'll see you back here at four tomorrow, for our first session?' asks Mrs Boland, and I can't for the life of me remember what I have agreed to.

At the first session Mrs Boland is waiting for us all and has placed her hands in her lap and made a little chapel out of them.

She has little low chappals she keeps sliding her feet out of like satin slippers; now and then she allows one to dangle dangerously on one of her toes, the nails of which are painted the colour of fresh peaches (exactly what I would expect from a woman like her).

'Call me Rowena,' says Mrs Boland at the beginning of our session. She remembers I am in the class. 'I mean think of me as Rowena, of course – could you do that? Ruby?'

I nod slowly. Mrs Boland gives us a handout. It's called 'How Molehills Can Become Mountains', and contains some real-life personal examples of catastrophisation:

— The time I left the small window open in the attic and imagined a tiny burglar gained entry into the house. (They didn't.) (Millicent, aged 72)
— The time I drove to the cinema and thought I hadn't put my handbrake on, and imagined the parked car lurching forward into the one ahead. (It didn't.) (Jack, aged 62)

— The time I had a cough for over two months, and I imagined being resistant to all forms of antibiotics and contracting gangrene in my lungs, coughing up blood, and dying slowly and painfully, intubated in a hospice. (I didn't!) (Dawn, aged 67)

She introduces us to her next session, 'The Three Types of Jeopardy', and passes us all a worksheet. There's a hand-drawn diagonal line which represents a seesaw. At the bottom of the seesaw, next to the word *magnification*, is a drawing of a girl seated on the seesaw, gripping the equipment tightly with a sad/worried face. On the other end, high up on the seesaw, is a little boy sliding dangerously off his seat, his hands flung up in the air and framed in an ecstatic pose. Next to him is the word *minimisation*.

We study this diagram, and even colour it in or embellish it as we choose. I spend the rest of the session staring at the little girl with her little hat, perfectly balanced on her little seesaw seat, and admire how she had been drawn so symmetrically.

In the next exercise there are a bunch of words in a box which we can sort into the two categories:

DRUG-TAKING / AGORAPHOBIA / PARACHUTING / THEFT / UNPROTECTED SEX / RECLUSIVENESS / MAKING FRIENDS / SPEAKING / TRAVELLING / SLEEPING / CHANGE / CLIMBING / LIVING / VIOLENCE / UNIVERSITY

The last word is in a different font from the others, which makes me think she has inserted it at the last minute for my benefit. I look at all the other members of the group, who have already started on the exercise. Mrs Boland gives me an encouraging nod. I quickly sort the words into two columns and wait for the others to finish. It strikes me that if I rearrange and attach some connectives to the words, they would make the headline 'Drug-taking, Agoraphobic, Reclusive, Violent Girl Speaks' or, better still, 'A Parachuting, Living Girl Changes After Unprotected University Sex'.

Sophie, who's sitting next to me, takes a look at what I've done and starts laughing. Our eyes meet and I can't help smiling and when Mrs Boland comes over and looks at our work she says, 'As neither of you are finding these exercises very useful you may be excused and wait outside.' I can see she must finally be at the end of her therapising thread.

Outside, Sophie and I sit on the steps. Sophie offers me a cigarette.

I decline at first but then she offers again, so I take the skinny stick and inhale slightly, but not competently enough and Sophie snatches the cigarette away from me in dismay. Sophie is in Mrs Boland's special group with me because she has serious anger issues. I knew Sophie had anger issues so naturally she spoke in a slightly combative but obsessed tone whilst she took long lugs on the cigarette.

'You know, my parents have a room filled with books but not one of them tells the truth. That's why I don't bother learning. And I am not going to give that bitch Boland any satisfaction in trying to cure me out of it. I am not interested in smearing my guts all over a page with a palette knife for her satisfaction.'

Sophie's father was a university lecturer. Her mother was also a brilliant academic in the subject of epistemology and ethics but was declining rapidly after she had contracted a disease she caught from a bite of a black-legged tick living in the fur of a deer.

I liked Sophie, I liked the way she spoke so clear and loud, never hesitating, her brain quickly pulsing out thoughts, so they came out like pellets of hail. But then my mind rested on Farah again and how I thought I knew her all these years and how she had closed the door in my face, and I tried to stamp all over my impulses. I had never met anyone like Sophie before.

'I know what they all say about me,' she continued, reading my thoughts, 'that I have it better than most, that I am ungrateful, and need to take a look around and get some perspective.' That was exactly what they said about her, to be fair, so I nodded quickly.

She put her hand in her pocket and withdrew a notebook. Its cover was thick and black and old like it might contain ancient spells and runes.

'This is where I put everything,' she said, crouching lower and whispering conspiratorially in my ear.

And for the hundredth time this month I felt a desire to steal an object, to feel it in my hand and hold its Bible-weight importance.

As Sophie moved forward, I could see long marks on her forearm, and at the top something resembling a crop circle, precisely drawn like she'd used a compass or a child's bangle to draw around. I wonder why a pen was not enough. Why did she have to indelibly mark herself and cause the pain when she was already in pain? I wonder if actually she had been in her parents' library after all and had decided to painstakingly replicate some runic inscriptions from a Swedish book on early art onto her arm with a blade. Maybe not everything was about mothers. Sophie might be worried about a lot of things but right here, with me, with her bad arms and her fleshy thighs pressed against mine, she just seemed floppy and desperate, and I wanted so much to take her head in my arms and stroke her wild, choppy hair till she went fuzzy with feeling and fell asleep like I used to do in my mother's wardrobe.

Mrs Boland comes out and sits beside us. Sophie is scowling. I make room for her on the door sill.

'Well, girls, let's go back inside and try our next exercise.'

MOLEHILLS

The time when I was four and my father was on a night shift, and my mother woke us and told us that a snake was hidden in our bedclothes, and stood ready to strike with something called a gandasa (a mini-bladed, long-handled scythe that you use to chop stubborn brambles). (She didn't.)

The time she decided to plant in the garden by moonlight, and wouldn't come back inside. (She did.)

The time of the dream in which my mother and I are standing in the deep well of a train track. Waiting commuters are sprawled everywhere on platforms. A train is approaching in the half-dark; we see its bright lights leaving the tunnel, coming towards us. 'The train is coming, we need to move to the platform,' I say to my mother, but my mother shakes her head. I try to pull her up but my mother refuses to move — she's looking at the lights, and as I scramble off the platform the light envelops my mother. (It's just a dream. I wake up.)

EENA IS DEAD

Eena had gone on to the other side. Eena was in a better place. Eena had gone to meet her maker and was resting forever. Eena had climbed the stairway to Heaven and been delivered to God; she was in his hands. Eena had slipped away and been carried on the angel's wings to everlasting peace. Eena was playing the harp in the eternal light. Eena had departed and was no more. Eena had reached a negative outcome. Eena had passed on. Eena was a lonely passenger overflowing her lustrous boundaries at the gates of a bloom-filled heaven. Eena was standing barefoot on the overburdened lanes of Calcutta; she was hustling her way to the other side of the road. And who knows what's on the other side of the road? Maybe the ocean, maybe the forest with its collection of roosting tree sparrows waiting for Eena, their cryptic mouths wide open.

EENA IS DEAD

It was September. They were behind with the pond. It nearly existed – there was a large hole in exactly the right place – but they were behind with the pond.

Alfred came to the front of the house. He never came to the front door, apart from one time when he brought me specialist books about the Great War, oversized encyclopaedias with ancient ochre maps folded into their bellies.

'It's the hospitals that kill you in the end,' Alfred always says. 'They kill you because the doctors don't love the patients like they should do.'

The relationship of our two families existed in the garden's borders, on the edges of the lawn, or under the buddleia's overhang, or under the shadeless elm tree (dying, almost dead), and only then when the garden was alive, in spring, in summer.

Of course, bumping into Alf occasionally outside the garden was unavoidable, and I had seen him in foreign locations such as the local shops, and once in the library, but I always had a compulsion to hide, which I managed to do successfully.

Alfred was at our door and Eena, it turned out, was next door in the kitchen, dead in her deckchair. I followed my father to the Parkers' house. A single bulb swung above her face, the light soft and brilliant on Eena's long body. She was spread out biblically in her chair in her brown housecoat; her toothless mouth was open wide. My father dutifully checked her pulse.

'She's gone then, has she?' said Alfred desultorily.

My father turned to look at Alfred and nodded. Alfred looked so tired and so old and I felt a little sting. I knew right then that there was never going to be a pond.

'I wondered if I could use your phone to call the doctors?' said Mr Parker.

My father nodded sadly. We all walked back to our sitting room. Alfred retrieved a small black address book from his jacket, and we gathered around the phone like it was a fire. My father helped him dial the numbers whilst Eena lay quietly next door in her chair.

INSTRUCTIONS FOR LIVING

At the next session with Rowena Boland it's all about giving and sharing. We are drafting a list of helpful things, a resource list containing useful tips for gloom-filled days, when you're at your lowest and need a stab of joy. I like the idea of this. I think I could happily draft a little list of an aphoristic nature that could be like a jolt of sunshine when the days are blue-black.

1. The first sign of madness is not talking to yourself – sometimes it's the sanest thing you can do. (Thereby offering reassurance.)
2. Attachment is overrated. (Non-judgemental advice to the lonely, the friendless, the dispossessed.)
3. Don't talk to pigeons. (This is the sanest thing not to do as pigeons are themselves insane, being the most revolutionary of birds, plus they carry vast amounts of infectious disease.)
4. Never take your pulse with your thumb. (This can give you a very misleading reading.)
5. Every day say one positive thing about yourself. Better still, write down thirty-one positive things on a piece of paper, one for every day of the month, and some left over for the more fretful days, then

screw them into little balls and leave them in a box or drawer. Breathe deeply from your core before taking them out, looking in the mirror and reading the message to yourself eyeball to eyeball.

'My destiny is life.'

'I am worthy of this day.'

'I am as beautiful as the chain of mountains in my heart.'

'Every moment lived in happiness is a gift to the soul.'

'I am, I am, I am.' Etc. etc.

It suddenly hits me that this may be deeply counter to the self-help project Mrs B had in mind, because most people who suffer from depression are at their worst in the season of spring (April being the cruellest month) because of the disparity between their feelings and the burgeoning beauty and hope sprouting in the natural world all around them. It could be that the compounding emptiness after standing in front of the mirror repeating banal adjectives such as *beauty* and *worthy* would just sharpen the sadness, and eventually annihilate the soul or, worse, trigger an episode of trauma.

I spend the rest of the session chewing the top of my pen, thinking all these things over. I try really hard to poke at my mind for anything else and nothing offers itself up, so I obliterate all the other words, until I am just left with:

'Don't talk to pigeons'

screaming like a siren on the page. I hand it in anyway and try to think of ways I can avoid another session.

EENA'S COLLECTION

They collected old Eena up. The doctor eventually came and then the undertaker who zipped her up in a skinny long bag and carried her into the back of a black van. Rania was watching from the window.

'How do they know it's Eena?' my sister asks. 'How do they know she's actually dead?'

'They just know these things. They can check before they zip her up.'

'What if she just has a very low heartbeat, or she's in a coma and they can't tell? The doctor doesn't have any equipment and machines with him to check for certain.'

'I think she seemed dead.' My father looks towards me. 'You saw her, Ruby – didn't she look dead?'

I nod slowly and seriously, like I'm an expert on how a dead person should be. I can tell that my sister is really annoyed that I got there first and saw a real live dead body before she did, and that's never going to change even if she sees a hundred more dead people now.

EENA IS DEAD

Eena was in fact not quite dead in all respects, because no one had the heart to tell my mother. My mother was having a good few days; she was eating, and she was humming a tune that no one knew the words to; her hair had been swept up and tied into a bun, her flyaway hairs at the front secured with hair grips. This gave her face a slightly older but more serene appearance, and as a result she appeared straighter when she walked, her arms less floppy and her gait more precise. All in all, she was a sharper presence in the room. My father was not about to ruin it by telling her the truth about Eena. All the circumstances alluded to it, but my father wanted to spare her one day more, then another day, until finally he could not find the words to say it. Hindus believe that the soul of the dead floats around the family for thirteen days watching loved ones mourn and grieve and then, once it has soaked up and is saturated with all their salty tears it finally departs, making its long journey to its final destination.

The day of the funeral came, and my father tried to stealthily leave the house on his own. Rania had tried in vain to intervene and put a stop to the nonsense.

'For God's sake, Dad, it's worse the more you delay it.'

'When will we do it, then?'

'You will just make it worse and worse; you are burying Eena today. I am sure even she will work it out.'

'Yes, yes, but not yet, wait till she's a little stronger.' *Soon*, my father would say.

Just before he set off for the funeral, we found our father wringing his hat in his hands in the hallway. He had banned all of us from attending, but he was already teary-eyed from having to face the whole event on his own.

'Let sleeping dogs lie,' my father said, shutting my sister down before she said any more, and closing the front door behind him.

But the truth was my mother didn't want to work it out. When my father left for the funeral, I spied on my mother upstairs; she was moving fluidly around the bedrooms, putting away clothes, carrying books to shelves, humming a light insect buzz. Maybe she even knew where our father was going. But the situation of Eena's death had been dodged, swerved around like a roadkill animal you never have to look back at, though you know deep down you heard the gentle thud of the creature. The fact of it was neglected, and if you put your mind in another place perhaps death itself could be avoided like this, sadness and mourning dispensed with. Who's to say what's alive or dead, some might say that as long as one living thing still imagines another to be living, they are alive.

So yes, Eena remained alive. Eena had found her immortal home in my mother's mind.

THE POND

My father doesn't mention the pond again. He secretly hopes my mother will not dwell on it and might be distracted by something else. The problem with this rationale is that the garden was her main distraction from life and without the main distraction there is just life that she needed to be distracted from in the first place. No attempt is made to fill in the sad would-be-pond hole. Around it lies all the paraphernalia for pond world-building. Everything is still strewn around the shoreline: the tools, the hessian, the water-loving plants in the wheelbarrow. The rubber liner for the pond has been left folded on the grass and will eventually degrade and crack, and when it's lifted up it will have sowbugs and small worms collecting and breeding in the yellowed grass. The irregular hole that's been dug at different depths will soften and erode and begin to attract the wrong sort of insects.

My father washes the dishes and wipes down the surfaces, and Rania sets out the breakfast.

'The garden is a fucking mess.' My mother isn't wrong about this, but we ignore her comment and my father begins boiling the kettle. I reach for a word in the silence.

'It's still a beautiful garden apart from the pond, just like you wanted it,' says my father calmly, eventually.

'I never said I wanted a beautiful garden, when did I ever say that?'

My father places the mug in front of her, but my mother is not touching anything with her hands and uses the backs of her wrists to push the cup away. If only we could have made her a pond. But I didn't know where to start. A pond is a wild and ungovernable thing and who knows what manner of creatures live in it. From where she is sitting, next to the kitchen window, you can see the true sadness of the garden but framed, illuminated, through the glass.

EENA
(FROM THE OTHER SIDE)

I suppose you could call them balconies; yes, let's call them many balconies balancing on clouds.

What can I tell you? That it hurts? No. Breathing, no. A little like flying, but the slow, wingless kind. Unsleeping-very-awake-feeling.

My barnacled mind returned to me, surfaces smoothed out. My thinking distilled. Quiet – yes – not lonely. All my fears captured, tamed and swept up tidily into a corner once again, manageable, harmless. Ahead of me tall grasses and voices, smells, familiar but like frayed seams of my dreams mended, crystalline.

I can tell you something important; that I have all the unbroken things about me. I have my great-grandmother's watch on my wrist, the one I lost at the swimming baths decades ago. Although it's not really a wrist it's on, I wear it nonetheless. Then my parents' magnolia floor lamp that I shattered by accident, the glass panels through which the light would throw all sorts of angles of colour on the kitchen floor when I was a little girl. An earliest image? A memory come back to me, probably.

That fine enamel box of mine that was taken away, the one full of buttons I used to like counting — my father used to say there was no harm in it, but my mother took against it.

What's to be gained from a girl that spends so much time counting wee buttons all day long?

Counting and stacking them up, the small tics of pleasure on my face, matching them up over and over like some sort of languid sickness.

My mother didn't want me to play with dolls — frivolous and shallow, she called them — and so I never did. But then she didn't like the way I was content with so little. I never quite understood what I was supposed to settle for instead. That was the way it was, you could never ask *why*, you had to work it out in between the gaps, in the silence between each careful mouthful of chewing the Sunday dinner, or run your fingertips along the wallpaper and underneath the ageing drawer-liners in the bedrooms.

Like that time I introduced her to Alf.

'Well that's fine, Eena, if that's who you've settled for,' she said in the kitchen on the morning of my wedding, with a faint scent of betrayal, though I could never understand how I could have disappointed her so much, if I had never been shown another way.

What I do have, and you do not have, is time. Time to think about opening up all these boxes around me that flow in noiselessly.

Now I have my button box back. I don't have everything, yet, but I hope you find it a touch reassuring that everything comes back eventually, all the broken things, the wept-over things come back, as if some gigantic magnet conjures them so they begin streaming back to you, the steady flow of metal filings.

I receive the babies, of course. I love their delicate nails. There are so many babies, but they pass through very quickly; they have no boxes to open so why should they wait?

I think of my boy, of course I do. Not him as that man, but before. How I prayed and craved for him. I couldn't stop shivering when he was born. He was a flower. His head so heavy. His head flopping over my chest like an unstaked, oversized sunflower, so large it was touch-and-go with the forceps. It was a miracle. All those false starts, babies bleeding away too early and as a midwife there was no way of hiding, though in the end when a baby finally held on I told no one at all; I couldn't hide it in the ward.

And then the day he came, one day of pushing and the consultant arriving and saying, 'Eena, you know the drill: we are going to have to do the cut.' In truth I wanted it. I wanted to feel everything, the searing pain of the incision along the perineum. Later, the midwives said that they had never heard a woman in a delivery room scream like that. I screamed like an animal. It was one of the hottest nights but still they had to close the windows or the visitors would have got distressed. Then when I wouldn't stop haemorrhaging Alf was beside himself.

'Save the mother – if there's any doubt, save her life.' He kept repeating it like a mantra.

Maybe that was the start of it – too much love for me and not enough for the new baby; the baby didn't hear a prayer or his mother's love-moan, he heard his mother's blood-curdling scream followed by his father's curse and that's why it all turned out so bad.

'Don't blame me, God,' I used to say when he started to turn out so bad and I knew, just knew – a mother always knows her child – and then I prayed to the Almighty: 'Give me strength. I am just a mother and after all you made me a mother and I tried my best to love him.'

As I said, there are so many boxes. But this here one reminds me of the wildness of that night, when they ripped the baby out of me and gave me my boy, laid my beautiful clean boy on my chest.

THE SON

Three days later Mr Parker died of a broken heart.

One day after that the Parkers' son knocked at our door. My father ushered him in and gave him the spare keys and the papers for his parents' house.

It was the first time we had seen the Parkers' son. He was an oversized man who owned and ran a taxi firm on the Isle of Wight and had a sideline in driving lessons. He sat in our living room and cried loudly for several moments, then he went quiet and drank his tea and finished the entire plate of cashew nuts. He thanked my father.

'You have a lovely family,' the big man said, 'such good quiet girls.' His small, intense eyes followed my mother around the room as she carried the plates, and my mother looked down at the carpet instinctively like an ancient cord had been pulled at the front of her head. Finally, he licked his lips and moved his gaze towards me, and I found myself protectively crossing my arms over my new little breasts.

Mr Parker's son lived in his parents' house for three months. Rania came back one afternoon and told me to stay the hell away from him, that the Parkers' son was the kind of man who you might be justified in killing. Rania stopped lying in the garden on a blanket in a pair of tiny shorts and crop top.

But I already knew the Parkers' son was a bad man by the way he manoeuvred the car out of the drive, gripping the steering wheel so tight whilst simultaneously clenching his teeth, like his molars were grinding up bones into paste.

ALFRED

I will miss Alfred Parker more than I can say. I will miss his kind eyes and his steadfastness. I will also miss his truth-telling, because plants and gardens and peat don't lie. I will miss all his essential truisms captured in phrases such as, 'Limey soil always fails to hold the nutrients well enough, so it doesn't matter what you feed them in the long run.' Or, 'A baby tree's fibrous roots need the wind to bend them this way and that. Most people overstake their saplings because they are trying to protect them, but you have to practise tough love with a tree.'

But underneath those words was something else. As Mr Parker knelt on his cushion and wiped the sweat from his brow with his sleeve after the effects of the overzealous sunshine, I could see that he had a secret, a heartache which he carried with him, heavy as a log.

V

I wait and wait for Rania. In the end I find her on the benches outside the park, alone. There's something wild about her, her teeth chattering with cold, her eyes spilling with tears over and over. She doesn't want to talk but lets me hold her hand. Finally, she takes a deep breath.

'Ruby, I just want to lie down and sleep. Take me home.'

I always thought that if something really bad happened to Rania I would know. Some hair trigger in my body might set off an alarm, the platelets in my blood would begin to quiver, somehow my body would message me. But nothing. My stupid, useless body. I went back to the exact time that Rania was in the house with Mr Parker's son. Where was I? In the garden? In my room, testing out mouth gestures in front of the mirror?

I willed myself to sleep. I kept thinking of all the things I didn't want anymore. In my bedroom there were still all the familiar things that make up a girl's room, but I no longer wanted furry bears holding hearts that were sewn onto their fur paws, or even the pale cotton bedcovers washed into softness. Everything looked wrong, like it was some other girl's room. I used to have a medium-sized doll. I had named her Pinky because of her light pink jumpsuit and fuchsia hairband and socks. I played with her and loved her, until one day from the shelf she winked and scared me. I put her in a box. I coffined her up in a box and slid her underneath the bed, so I didn't have to look at her. All was fine for a few days until something woke me up from my sleep, a small powder-touch hand lightly pressed my forehead, testing my body temperature. I knelt down and retrieved the box but the doll, clever as she was, had popped herself back, lightning quick. I decided to conduct a little blessing over the box. I crafted a curse-prayer and uttered the words softly but with conviction into the cold air of the room. Some things need to be uttered — all curses, certain prayers — a whisper will do. At this small funeral what did I say? A concoction of words from the garden, something like a potion, with magical and dark intent, all the grass names I knew at the time, the yew tree, the dying elms, those bad-sounding words beginning with V: *venal, verrucose, virgin*. I added the word *vulva* because it went nicely with *vetch*, strong, earthly words which accreted dark power. And when it was all done, I suddenly understood that I hadn't done it right. Any loved thing needs a funeral. All that energy has to go somewhere, after all; things that are loved need attending to in death. So, I gave my doll Pinky a kiss on the lips. I said goodbye and gave her her dues and her funeral rites, and she never disturbed me again.

It is late, and I go and check on Rania. She's sleeping quietly on her side and I curl up beside her. Rania is a messy sleeper who heats up in her bed; in the summer she likes to slip under the sheets with nothing on, and our father gets embarrassed and says, 'Rania, please don't do this anymore, what if there is an emergency in the middle of the night? A fire or a burglary or some other problem.'

But now Rania has her bedcovers twisted around her, her hair open and messed up around the pillow, and she looks like the little girl she once was in the photograph downstairs.

I curl up beside her and she wakes instantly and turns towards me.

'It's OK, Rubes, don't be scared. I am all right.'

But even the way she says this makes me scared, as if everything has shifted; her eyes look different and watery like they've been spiked with needles. I can see a dark rash on her throat and suddenly I know everything, that there are other red patches on her body that she'll try to hide, parts that will turn blue and curdle to yellow and eventually fade. And I don't know why but I start looking for them, trying to pull up her T-shirt.

'No, no, Ruby, stop it — I will tell you everything,' and she turns me over and pins me down till I nod my assent.

These are the things she told me:

1. He was the kind of man who fed dead flies to his cat.
2. That sick little yellow kitchen.
3. 'We could make this nice and respectful, drink from the good glasses not the bottle,' he said.
4. That it was forty-five minutes long, as long as a driving lesson.
5. There were shiny new brass bolts on the Parkers' door.
6. *'You are all liars.'*
7. All the clocks in all the rooms were perfectly in time.

8. She could see the simple frame of our bedroom window through the window glass.
9. *'Why does a swine need a pearl necklace?'*
10. *'The problem is that no one respects anyone anymore.'*
11. 'You ungrateful bitch.'

He said
come in
I am looking for my car keys
come in
and I said I will just wait right here in the hall
I gave him the set of spare keys in the envelope
but he was already deep inside the house and still talking
and so I stepped into the old house
the ageing yellow walls the low dado rail in the hall
and followed his voice into that sick little kitchen
where he was opening a bottle of gin or maybe vodka
something clear and cheap
pouring out a drink
one for me and one for you he said
and I say I don't drink I don't think so
and he said I know you drink and it's OK
I won't tell and I am leaving tomorrow
back to the grindstone
I am just finishing packing and so I laugh and say OK
I will have a little glass and he said that's good
good girl I won't tell your folks sit down he said
pointing towards the small two-seater couch

but I stayed standing in that sick little kitchen
and he went out and came back in and said
in a different voice
sit down
listen
everyone needs a drink before a driving lesson
and I laughed and said I'm not having a driving lesson
and he said the problem is that no one listens anymore
there's no respect and that gets lots of people into trouble
and I said I think I should go now
and I put down the glass on the kitchen counter
and he said you're not going anywhere missy
you are going to drink your drink on the sofa
because I have done my homework see
I know about the good ones and the bad ones
because in the end that's all a girl's got one thing
in the end and that's their reputation and you're a bad one
because I've done my research and asked enough questions
around here and by now I was crying
Ruby by now I knew this man what this man was
and what he was going to take from
me that I could try to make a run for it real quick
but then when I looked towards the door he had somehow bolted
it they must have been new bolts shiny new brass bolts
on the door and he is a big man Ruby and I swallowed
the sick that came up through my throat and
he said you can make it easy on yourself or I can be
a bad man to you and your body I could hurt you
tear you
he said you understand I could do all those things

or we could try to make this nice
we could drink from the good glasses
not the bottle
all respectful and you could pretend to be my girl
and it would be nice and clean and respectful
he said
and I wanted to fight
I wanted to
but I made my body dead
and I made my mind dead
Ruby
and drank a little more to deaden the pain
and he kept on like this
said it's up to you and the more he drank
the louder he got and finally he said
get upstairs or we do it right here
so I climbed the stairs him pushing me up
from behind
and he said you're driving this all the while
and all the different clocks in the rooms on the wall
each one perfectly in time because this was a man that liked to
    know the time
a man who took his time and
you wanted this he said
you made this possible and
I like a woman who takes control and
he patted the old Parkers' bed I thought to myself
how late it was
but it was only forty-five minutes long
as long as a driving lesson and after

I looked over through the window and there
was the simple frame of my bedroom window
Ruby just next door and afterwards
there was the bathroom across the hall
the one that still had a chain for the old-fashioned toilet
and that shitty carpet on the floor and then
he said come back here I want to show you something
and he opened up his wallet and put a finger in the slit of
the leather to slide out a photograph of a boy
around seven years old and I don't know
why I said this
I said, he's cute your son
he's sweet
I waited for him to say I can go now
I put my trainers on and he said of course
he said you came looking for me, didn't you?
So now you found me he said now you know.

DROWNINGS

Rania told me this last thing in a whisper, half inside her head and half outside, and then I touched her lightly on the shoulder and she curled up demurely towards the wall.

I make a meal and bring it up to her bed. She sits up and makes an effort, nibbles at the waffle, stirs the beans around and around the plate anticlockwise till they're cold. I break up the bread and try to place morsels of food into her mouth, but she shakes her head.

I put extra sugar in her mug of tea, because I saw someone do it in a documentary after someone's grandmother died, and she drinks this slowly. We are so badly made us human beings, our fleshy parts, our extremities, fingers and toes, our lips, but if Rania could survive one hour then she could maybe survive one more hour and another after that, and then she could survive another day and night. Victims of near drownings, and refugees who are pulled from the sea, don't die from the first drowning. They die from secondary drowning when everyone is less vigilant and they lie down to rest and drown in the water that's been hiding in air sacs in the lungs. Cancer patients frequently die from secondary tumours, like Nigel Dmitry's dad, who everyone said was cured and who went back to normal life working in the post office. One day we went in and he wasn't there. His wife told us that they found secondaries and the disease was cruel. He later died quickly of something on the liver.

That night as Rania slept I watched her, and I felt the studs of my heart come away. I heard the sound of an exhausted fly buzzing lightly around the room. I had no desire to kill this fly – yesterday I was another person and that Ruby would have slammed it across the windowpane, registered its convulsing body, then flipped its crushed parts out of the window. But right now I don't wish to participate in any way in its death or life. If I could I would like to de-encounter this fly in decline, but now . . . you see what's happened, like some slick trick the fly has played, the creature is in my head. The opposite thing. Like magic the fly has crawled its way in through some sudden fissure, this stealthy, terrible intruder.

AMAN

Kirsty's parents were not uninterested in her education; she had tennis lessons, and made a speech in assembly for the WWF, and was quite efficient at pestering everyone to sign her petitions. When she found out a Year 7's brother had leukaemia, she went around to all the classes with a tin for money for the family so they might be able to afford to go to Disney World. In each class she made a moving little prepared speech about charity peppered with Christian proverbs, including, 'There but for the grace of God go I.'

She chose her boyfriends carefully, her clothes tastefully, and she didn't really concern herself with friends because no one was going to meet her standards. On the odd occasion Rita might be used as a fill-in and appear at her side though she was stupid as a goat. Or Davina, who was half-half but didn't really look it, and was the most glamorous girl in the school because she had high tits and had worn tampons since she was eleven. Then there was David, of course. David, stupid, stupid David.

This new boy, Aman, was going to be Kirsty's undoing. Aman was an interesting new creature for Kirsty, because although he was undeniably brown his beauty indemnified him from this and all other faults he might possess. He was tall and wore a cricket jumper when it wasn't summer. His parents played golf and took him out of school for skiing. His mother wore miniskirts. Aman's allure was amplified by the fact that he was going to be a temporary exotic departure for Kirsty, though his glossy, golden skin colour was not Indian, really, more olive Greek; his floppy hair smelt of coconuts and sunshine and Kirsty knew that even the teachers noticed his beauty. Kirsty was determined to have him.

YOUR DAUGHTER KIRSTY
IS SCREWING
A PAKI. HIS NAME IS
AMAN SOLANKI.

I had tried out a different combination of words, but in the end, it seemed to me that the point of the letter was to express coldly and convey clearly the facts of the situation. 'Screwing' was politer than 'fucking', which seemed a bit crass, and expressions such as 'sleeping with' or 'going out with' had a prudish quality and would leave too much room for movement in the reader's mind.

I went to the post box and counted to five and pushed it through the slit.

THE TWENTY-FIRST
OF JUNE

It was Brian's birthday; the back door was open. This was a day on which Brian reflected on how many things had changed in his neighbourhood.

The airport used to have only one runway, you could leave your back door open and there was no need to pause and wait for the passing of supersonic planes that made the edges of your mind jangle. The children were white and courteous and had clear, pronounceable English names. There definitely used to be more beauty and more sunshine on the twenty-first of June.

When the Saturday-morning post arrived Brian nearly choked on his breakfast toast. The letter fell onto his lap and he lifted it forensically with two fingers, placed it on the kitchen table and spread it out.

'What's this?' he repeated, waggling his free hand around as he shoved the paper towards Kirsty. Brian had always suspected there was something wild and transgressive deep in the heart of his stepdaughter.

Waves of shock spread hotly through her body as she read then reread the letter.

'It's a lie,' she said in her small, plaintive, back-of-her-body voice.

'Do you know what I want to know?' Brian was talking very slowly. 'I want to know how we managed to raise such a fucking perverted daughter.'

Kirsty turned to her mother who winced just as Brian stood up and punched his stepdaughter, sending her reeling over to the other side of the floor.

GIRL

All the way back on the bus ride the empty pocket of my jacket was seeping out its disgust. I felt hot and conspicuous and guilty. But also, I felt exhilarated, powerful and ungovernable — the perfect conditions for psychopathy to flourish. In the windows of the bus my eyes surprised me, looking like cool, glassy pebbles and not the eyes of a frightened cat. I wanted to go home and scrub every part of my body, like the expensive murderesses do in art-house films before they themselves are strangulated by their lovers with their own suede belts or silk scarves. I wanted to be clean, but I also wanted to stay with the filth, stand in the wuthering dirt of it all. I wanted to feel this way; I didn't want to feel this way.

When I wake, I do a quick inward check of myself. I feel something is tightening and then releasing in my stomach. I put my feet on the floor, and they look as if they are floating.

I know that a line has been crossed. Even if no one else finds out I will carry this like a secret adulterer. If I were an adulteress at least there would be sharing of the guilt with another human being. I belonged to a new club, a club with the rest of the sinners, the ones who Popes excommunicated, the ones that get stoned in markets, and the ones who got tipped off tall buildings.

DISAPPEARANCES

The next day I went to the hairdresser and asked her to cut my hair off. *Eleven inches of hair off,* I wrote clearly in my notebook and showed the receptionist.

She scrutinised the photograph that I'd cut out of a magazine, and then told me she needed to check with her manager.

'Why don't we do something a little less drastic?' she suggested. 'What about a nice chin-length bob instead, something that might suit your face more?' She wanted me to understand before she took my money that I was contracting to annihilate my God-given femininity by this act. However, I had prepared for this resistance and made a big thing of smiling idiotically with my teeth and pointing to the cut-out picture in an enthusiastic way. Although the girl from the magazine looked nothing like me, she was still wearing foundation and highlighter on the angular parts of her face that gave her glow, and she had nude glossy paint on her lips, and that seemed to satisfy the staff that despite the radical haircut I so desired I was still pursuing beautification as a goal.

The hairdresser tied a low ponytail, the scissors yawned open and she cut. Just seconds later she had the long dark thing in her hands and asked if I wanted to keep it. I shook my head, didn't even want to look at it, truthfully, so she put it in a plastic bag and said, 'Well, some little girl might be able to use it, this is good, thick hair, Indian virgin hair, the best kind,' and she put the thing that was no longer any part of me in a drawer, which was good because by then it was making me sick looking at it in her hands.

On the way home the bus driver thought I was a boy at first. I read about a woman once who fell down and hit her head and when she awoke, she could only speak in perfectly accented French. It was strange sitting there on this jerky, half-empty bus, light-headed and lucid all at once. I took out my little notebook and wrote the word 'parallel' and then let the pen write the word 'Mum' and I felt tears squatting outside the door of my eyes.

It seemed to me that if I had undone my identity with a forty-minute haircut, and it was as easy as that, my identity must have been something quite ephemeral and unimportant in the first place. I sat on this bus and looked at the mothers with their precisely delineated toddlers and decided that this was yet another thing we had been duped about.

I quickly went upstairs and looked at my boyself in the mirror, and was less sure, wondering if I had made a mistake after all. I had a fragile, puppety look about me, and two dark patches of hair on the sides of my face were now exposed. I smiled into the mirror and the shock of my big white teeth set into my small face upset me. My eyes felt like heavy pits trying to press themselves inside my skull. I looked menacing and now there was nowhere to hide. My body-detective, the one who's normally so reliable and industrious, seemed to have fled the scene. I was entirely on my own.

GIRL

Rania tries in vain to re-feminise me, but I know I am too far gone. She brings out her bulging bag of jewellery and scarves in the vain hope of reviving my girl-self.

'Why?' she keeps asking me, 'why?' and I sit on the edge of my bed all sad and limp as she slaps me about, not hard, just to wake me up and make sure I'm listening to her. She gets close to me and rests her palms on my hand, and I can see the thin black flick of her eyeliner and the tiny baby hairs in the inner rim of her tear ducts.

'Did you do it yourself?' I shake my head, so then she starts blaming the 'fucking dodgy' hairdresser. 'How the hell did you even talk to them?'

I unfold the picture from the back of my jeans and she goes berserk.

'You stupid fucking idiot. They will think you are fucking insane. Wait, no . . . you are.' She holds out the magnifying mirror to make her point. I can't decide if I look worse or better than yesterday; my hair has been slept on and I hadn't noticed how roughly it has been chopped at the sides.

'There you go, see for yourself what a fucking mess you've made, you stupid selfish baby.' She's shouting, shoving the mirror towards me. 'Everything is not about you, Ruby, not every single thing.' Then Rania is crying again, quiet tears. We both sit side by side on the bed for a long time till the light falls away, until we are both sitting in the simple dark of the room and I feel a not unpleasant tingle along my spine as a part of me breaks off and much like a little spider it scuttles away into the darkness.

After she leaves the room, I lie down on my bed and slide under the duvet and my body clicks shut like a purse. I sleep for days. It seems like days, weeks, months. I steer my dreams along pavements and through wide tree-lined streets, walking, always walking. In one dream I am suddenly on a shoreline, a sandy, perfect beach, talking to the waves and they are talking back about mountains, about the incursions of sea snails and all things they've touched with their wave-fingers then – *switch*. I am alone and lit on a stage. I have brought with me one hundred and thirty-six words for snow and I have an audience; I am not at all frightened. I give them my snow similes, my aphorisms, long, pendulous monosyllabic words, hyphenated Latinate words. I speak into the well of dark silence. The audience is captivated and when I finish the set to applause I bow deeply and curtsey; people are throwing flowers. Long, dark stems with small, blood-red heads are landing at my feet. *More*, they shout, *more, more*.

THE VISIT

The room they put me in was a square room with low, neat little windows. On the table a plant, a grand white orchid. I touched a leaf this plant had grown, but it was not real — the plant had not sprouted the leaf or given the flower after all. I knew this discovery would appal you. You would say something like, 'How can they know anything about caring if they can't be bothered to tend to one live, living creature?' or words to that effect.

I have passed on my tiny folded notes to the nurses. The nurses slip them in their pockets, so I have written dozens. I keep writing them to you and supplying them to the staff in the hope that one will filter through and you will know that I am here waiting.

I would like to see my mother urgently.
 Please could you kindly ask my mother if she will see me?
 I would very much like to visit my mother.

Then later:

I am summoning all my strength to be patient and wait and be good and

I promise I will only keep her for a moment.
      Love Ruby.

They won't let me see you, yet. They don't say *no*, they don't
say *yes*. This is an intermediate room, a limbo room. With
my new hair I am limbo incarnate – neither this nor that,
here nor there. In this room there must be waiting, and from
time to time they come and look – I pass them another note
which they might take to you. The cleaner sweeps under my
feet without asking.

Your favourite words are *nature*, *plant*, *soil* and *bud*. One of
my favourite words for a long time was *glade*. I came across the
word for the first time in a fairy tale we once read together.
I liked the idea of *sitting in the glade in a forest* with you, where a
wedge of sunlight illuminated the forest floor close to a river-
bank, close enough to hear the water of a stream babbling,
a perfect place for a picnic, our backs leaning on an ancient
drystone wall covered with lichen.

They will not let me see you. I think it's because they detect
in my scent my desperation – I try to hide it, but animal fear
clings to me. They found my lucky pistol when they checked
my bag and now that's gone too. Perhaps you do not want to
see me? Because I will not leave, they call my father.

He arrives and looks relieved. 'We've been so worried
about you, Ruby. Poor you,' he says, sadly patting my shorn
head. As soon as he touches me my tears start falling and
they won't stop.

SNOW

My mother is late. My teacher stands outside the classroom, holding my hand and complaining that my mother is late again. All day there's been talk of snow. I am looking at the black metal gates that my mother might at any moment walk through. My teacher is talking but my eyes are fixed on the gate and its railings, which will allow me to catch sight of my mother as she approaches the school. I let my eyes follow the white lines of a netball court, crossed with other yellow lines that were probably for hockey, and yet another set of lines for a sport I didn't yet know the name of.

We wait. The playground empties. I'm cold and can no longer feel my feet; I haven't yet put on my gloves, though I'm sure they are safely sitting in a nest in one of my pockets. I am sure my mother will turn the corner at any moment and then I will slip my hand into my mother's hand and maybe even into her coat pocket. I close my eyes. I am old enough to know that if you want something badly enough, you're more likely to get it if you leave the room.

My teacher has stopped talking and is now walking me over to the gate. I open my eyes. I have conjured my mother. My mother's head is wrapped in a long green scarf. She listens to the teacher complaining to her, but my mother doesn't reply, so the teacher shrugs her shoulders and briskly heads back to the classroom. I place my hand into my mother's hand. The bus home is vibrating and overheated. The roads are overburdened with traffic and my mind is dulled into a stupor. My mother is also quiet but then she is crying, her beautiful bones are trembling. She is reading from a pale blue letter. I lean myself into my mother, press my body into her. I rest my cheek against her long hair. My mother turns away and whispers to herself by the window; her reflection floats above mine.

The sky is sagging downwards like a loose veil. All day there's been talk of snow. An old woman enters the bus, her hair lit with light flakes. She is making the sound that the very old make with the push of each breath out into the air.

I try to take the letter from my mother's hands. My mother clasps the top of my arms and squeezes so hard I let out a sound.

When it's time to leave the bus, I gather up my mother's shopping bags slumped by her feet and we both step off the bus into the snow.

Something on the shelf of my mother's heart died when she came to England. She suffered badly from chilblains, the gnawing pain. My father bought new shoes, but the stubborn leather pressed against the tender lumps on her toes and made her wince and cry when she walked.

The doctors prescribed pills for loneliness, pills for her purple toes, insomnia pills and pills for the tic she developed on her left eyebrow, which she had begun to pinch so hard she felt the water gushing out through her tear ducts.

ENDINGS

The mother sleeps. Mostly. The foxes still come and go. It's March but it's been snowing. Up until last week we were still leaving milk and chicken bones out for them; my father can't bear the sound of their suffering. Just last week he took us to visit our mother, our feet crunching the icy ground beneath us. They had taken her out of bed, and she was waiting for us patiently, her elbows scrubbed but dry with a bubbly texture. I reached over and touched one with my fingertips.

She holds my chin in her hands and tells me, *Sorry, sorry,* and that she loves me. I promise her I will turn her fuchsia plant on the patio when summer comes but that she'll be home before then.

We head back to the car. I look across and she is standing by the bay window, making slow and tranquil gestures with her hands. I think she is waving. I wave back.

ACKNOWLEDGEMENTS

I especially wish to thank my editor Tara Tobler for her passion and commitment to the project, who gently took the pulse of the book and tended to its heart valves with such care.

Thank you to Stefan and the team at *And Other Stories* for all their attention and making such a beautiful book.

This book would never have come into being without the generous support of some very astute readers, both poets and novelists. Those who helped with an initial steer include: Nathalie Teitler, Chris Emery and Sarah Corbett.

Further down the journey of the novel I am grateful for invaluable comments on the manuscript by Leo Boix, Shehnaz Suterwalla and special thanks to Martha Sprackland for her editing eyes.

Thank you to Maryam Najand for her sensitive listening to Ruby's voice in a hotel bar in Florence, 2019. Thank you also to Mimi Khalvati for friendship, wisdom and teaching me how to be a better writer.

Heartfelt thanks to Preti Taneja for her insight and being a vital early advocate for the book.

Thank you to my parents for my Monday writing days. I am grateful to my brother Sunnie who introduced me to different kinds of reading when I was growing up, my daughters Lily and Priya for putting up with my constant Ruby-related distractions, and Stephen for his reading and comments on the final version. To Aisha, thank you for your much valued friendship these past few years.

Thank you to my agent Tracy Bohan, and Jennifer Bernstein, who had faith in the book from the outset.

This book is for all the Rubys, everywhere.

Dear readers,

As well as relying on bookshop sales, And Other Stories relies on subscriptions from people like you for many of our books, whose stories other publishers often consider too risky to take on.

Our subscribers don't just make the books physically happen. They also help us approach booksellers, because we can demonstrate that our books already have readers and fans. And they give us the security to publish in line with our values, which are collaborative, imaginative and 'shamelessly literary'.

All of our subscribers:

- receive a first-edition copy of each of the books they subscribe to
- are thanked by name at the end of our subscriber-supported books
- receive little extras from us by way of thank you, for example: postcards created by our authors

BECOME A SUBSCRIBER,
OR GIVE A SUBSCRIPTION TO A FRIEND

Visit andotherstories.org/subscriptions to help make our books happen. You can subscribe to books we're in the process of making. To purchase books we have already published, we urge you to support your local or favourite bookshop and order directly from them – the often unsung heroes of publishing.

OTHER WAYS TO GET INVOLVED

If you'd like to know about upcoming events and reading groups (our foreign-language reading groups help us choose books to publish, for example) you can:

- join our mailing list at: andotherstories.org
- follow us on Twitter: @andothertweets
- join us on Facebook: facebook.com/AndOtherStoriesBooks
- admire our books on Instagram: @andotherpics
- follow our blog: andotherstories.org/ampersand

THIS BOOK WAS MADE POSSIBLE THANKS TO THE SUPPORT OF

A Cudmore
Aaron McEnery
Aaron Schneider
Abi Webb
Abigail Howell
Abigail Walton
Adam Clarke
Adam Lenson
Adrian Astur
  Alvarez
Adrián Perez
Aifric Campbell
Aisha McLean
Ajay Sharma
Alan Donnelly
Alan Felsenthal
Alan Stoskopf
Alastair Gillespie
Alastair Whitson
Albert Puente
Alex Fleming
Alex Lockwood
Alex Pearce
Alex Ramsey
Alexander Williams
Alexandra Stewart
Alexandra Stewart
Alexandra Tilden
Alexandra Webb
Alexandra Tammaro
Ali Ersahin
Ali Smith
Ali Usman
Alice Morgan
Alice Radosh
Alice Smith
Alice Toulmin
Alice Tranah
Alice Wilkinson
Alison Hardy
Alison Winston
Aliya Rashid
Alyssa Rinaldi
Amado Floresca
Amaia Gabantxo
Amalia Gladhart
Amanda
Amanda Dalton
Amanda Geenen
Amanda Maria
  Izquierdo
  Gonzalez
Amanda Read
Amber Da
Amelia Lowe
Amitav Hajra
Amy Benson
Amy Bessent
Amy Bojang
Amy Finch

Amy Kitchens
Amy Tabb
Ana Novak
Anastasía Carver
Andra Dusu
Andrea Barlien
Andrea Brownstone
Andrea Oyarzabal
  Koppes
Andrea Reece
Andrew Marston
Andrew McCallum
Andrew McDougall
Andrew Ratomski
Andrew Reece
Andrew Rego
Andy Corsham
Andy Turner
Angelica Ribichini
Angus Walker
Anita Starosta
Ann Rees
Anna French
Anna Gibson
Anna Hawthorne
Anna Milsom
Anna Zaranko
Anne Barnes
Anne Boileau Clarke
Anne Carus
Anne Craven
Anne Edyvean
Anne Kangley
Anne O' Brien
Anne Ryden
Anne Sticksel
Anne Withane
Annette Hamilton
Annie McDermott
Anonymous
Anonymous
Anthony Alexander
Antonia Lloyd-Jones
Antonia Saske
Antony Osgood
Antony Pearce
Aoife Boyd
Arabella Bosworth
Archie Davies
Aron Negyesi
Aron Trauring
Arthur John Rowles
Asako Serizawa
Ash Lazarus
Ashleigh Sutton
Audrey Mash
Audrey Small
Barbara Bettsworth
Barbara Mellor
Barbara Robinson

Barbara Spicer
Barry Norton
Bea Karol Burks
Becky Cherriman
Becky Matthewson
Ben Buchwald
Ben Schofield
Ben Thornton
Ben Walter
Benjamin Judge
Benjamin Pester
Beth Heim de Bera
Bethan Kent
Beverley Thomas
Bianca Duec
Bianca Jackson
Bianca Winter
Bill Fletcher
Björn Warren
Bjørnar Djupevik
  Hagen
Blazej Jedras
Briallen Hopper
Brian Anderson
Brian Byrne
Brian Conn
Brian Smith
Brigita Ptackova
Briony Hey
Buck Johnston
Burkhard Fehsenfeld
Caitlin Halpern
Caitriona Lally
Cameron Adams
Cameron Lindo
Camilla Imperiali
Campbell McEwan
Carla Ballin
Carla Castanos
Carole Parkhouse
Carolina Pineiro
Caroline Jupp
Caroline Perry
Caroline West
Catharine Braithwaite
Catherine Barton
Catherine Lambert
Catherine
  Williamson
Catherine Tandy
Cathryn Siegal-
  Bergman
Cathy Galvin
Cathy Sowell
Catie Kosinski
Catriona Gibbs
Cecilia Rossi
Cecilia Uribe
Chantal Lyons
Chantal Wright

Charlene Huggins
Charles Fernyhough
Charles Kovach
Charles Dee Mitchell
Charles Rowe
Charlie Levin
Charlie Small
Charlotte Bruton
Charlotte Coulthard
Charlotte Durnajkin
Charlotte Whittle
Charlotte Woodford
Cherilyn Elston
China Miéville
Chris Blackmore
Chris Holmes
Chris Johnstone
Chris Köpruner
Chris Lintott
Chris McCann
Chris Potts
Chris Stergalas
Chris Stevenson
Chris Thornton
Christian
  Schuhmann
Christina Moutsou
Christine Bartels
Christine Humphreys
Christopher Allen
Christopher Homfray
Christopher Smith
Christopher Stout
Ciara Ní Riain
Ciarán Schütte
Claire Adams
Claire Brooksby
Claire Mackintosh
Claire Morrison
Claire Smith
Claire Williams
Clare Young
Clarice Borges
Claudia Mazzoncini
Cliona Quigley
Colin Denyer
Colin Hewlett
Colin Matthews
Collin Brooke
Cornelia Svedman
Cortina Butler
Courtney Lilly
Craig Kennedy
Cynthia De La Torre
Cyrus Massoudi
Daisy Savage
Dale Wisely
Dan Martin
Dana Lapidot
Daniel Gillespie

Daniel Hahn
Daniel Hester-Smith
Daniel Jones
Daniel Oudshoorn
Daniel Stewart
Daniel Syrovy
Daniel Venn
Daniela Steierberg
Darina Brejtrova
Darryll Rogers
Dave Lander
David Anderson
David Coates
David Cowan
David Davies
David Gould
David Greenlaw
David Hebblethwaite
David Higgins
David Johnson-
 Davies
David Leverington
David F Long
David McIntyre
David and Lydia Pell
David Richardson
David Shriver
David Smith
David Thornton
Dawn Bass
Dean Stokes
Dean Taucher
Deb Hughes
Deb Unferth
Debbie Enever
Debbie Pinfold
Deborah Herron
Declan Gardner
Declan O'Driscoll
Deirdre Nic
 Mhathuna
Denis Larose
Denis Stillewagt &
 Anca Fronescu
Denise Bretländer
Denton Djurasevich
Desiree Mason
Diana Baker Smith
Diane Salisbury
Diarmuid Hickey
Dietrich Menzel
Dina Abdul-Wahab
Dinesh Prasad
Dominic Nolan
Dominick Santa
 Cattarina
Dominique Hudson
Dorothy Bottrell
Doug Wallace
Duncan Clubb

Duncan Macgregor
Duncan Marks
Dustin Hackfeld
Dyanne Prinsen
Earl James
Ebba Tornérhielm
Ed Tronick
Ekaterina Beliakova
Elaine Frances
Elaine Juzl
Eleanor Maier
Eleanor Updegraff
Elena Esparza
Elif Aganoglu
Elina Zicmane
Elisabeth Cook
Eliza Mood
Elizabeth Braswell
Elizabeth Coombes
Elizabeth Draper
Elizabeth Franz
Elizabeth Guss
Elizabeth Leach
Elizabeth Seals
Elizabeth Wood
Ellen Wilkinson
Ellie Goddard
Emily Armitage
Emily Dixon
Emily Jang
Emily Paine
Emily Webber
Emily Williams
Emma Bielecki
Emma Louise Grove
Emma Morgan
Emma Page
Emma Post
Eric Anderson
Erica Mason
Erin Cameron Allen
Esmée de Heer
Esther Donnelly
Esther Kinsky
Ethan Madarieta
Ethan White
Eugene O'Hare
Eunji Kim
Eva Oddo
Eve Corcoran
Ewan Tant
F Gary Knapp
Fawzia Kane
Fay Barrett
Felicity Williams
Felix Valdivieso
Finbarr Farragher
Fiona Mozley
Forrest Pelsue
Fran Sanderson

Frances Thiessen
Francesca Brooks
Francesca Hemery
Francesca Rhydderch
Francis Mathias
Frank Rodrigues
Frank van Orsouw
Frankie Mullin
Frauke Matthes
Freddie Radford
Friederike Knabe
Gabriel Colnic
Gabriel and Mary de
 Courcy Cooney
Gala Copley
Garan Holcombe
Gavin Aitchison
Gavin Collins
Gavin Smith
Gawain Espley
Gemma Doyle
Genaro Palomo Jr
Genevieve Lewington
Geoff Thrower
Geoffrey Cohen
Geoffrey Urland
George Stanbury
George Wilkinson
Georgia Shomidie
Georgia Wall
Georgina Norton
Gerry Craddock
Gill Boag-Munroe
Gillian Grant
Gina Heathcote
Glenn Russell
Gordon Cameron
Gosia Pennar
Grace Cohen
Graham Blenkinsop
Graham R Foster
Graham Page
Grant Rintoul
Gregory Philp
Hadil Balzan
Halina Schiffman-
 Shilo
Hamish Russell
Hannah Bucknell
Hannah Freeman
Hannah Harford-
 Wright
Hannah Jane
 Lownsbrough
Hannah Morris
Hannah Procter
Hannah Rapley
Hannah Vidmark
Hanora Bagnell
Hans Lazda

Harriet Stiles
Haydon Spenceley
Hayley Cox
Hazel Smoczynska
Heidi Gilhooly
Helen Moor
Helena Buffery
Henriette
 Magerstaedt
Henrike Laehnemann
Henry Patino
Holly Down
Howard Robinson
Hugh Shipley
Hyoung-Won Park
Iain Forsyth
Ian Hagues
Ian McMillan
Ian Mond
Ian Randall
Ian Whiteley
Ida Grochowska
Ines Alfano
Ingunn Vallumroed
Iona Stevens
Irene Croal
Irene Mansfield
Irina Tzanova
Isabella Garment
Isabella Weibrecht
Isabelle Schneider
Isobel Foxford
Ivy Lin
Jacinta Perez Gavilan
 Torres
Jack Brown
Jacqueline Haskell
Jacqueline Lademann
Jacqui Jackson
Jade Yiu
Jake Baldwinson
James Attlee
James Beck
James Crossley
James Cubbon
James Elkins
James Greer
James Kinsley
James Lee
James Lehmann
James Leonard
James Lesniak
James Leveque
James Portlock
James Scudamore
James Silvestro
Jamie Cox
Jamie Mollart
Jan Hicks
Jan Leah Lowe

Marja S Laaksonen
Mark Bridgman
Mark Huband
Mark Sargent
Mark Sheets
Mark Sztyber
Mark Walsh
Mark Waters
Marlene Simoes
Martin Brown
Martin Price
Martin Eric Rodgers
Mary Angela
  Brevidoro
Mary Heiss
Mary Wang
Maryse Meijer
Mathieu Trudeau
Matt Davies
Matt Greene
Matt O'Connor
Matthew Adamson
Matthew Armstrong
Matthew Banash
Matthew Black
Matthew Eatough
Matthew Francis
Matthew Gill
Matthew Lowe
Matthew Woodman
Matthias Rosenberg
Maura Cheeks
Maureen Cullen
Max Cairnduff
Max Longman
Meaghan Delahunt
Meg Lovelock
Megan Holt
Megan Taylor
Megan Wittling
Mel Pryor
Melissa Beck
Melissa Quignon-
  Finch
Melissa Stogsdill
Meredith Martin
Mia Khachidze
Michael Aguilar
Michael Bichko
Michael Boog
Michael James
  Eastwood
Michael Floyd
Michael Gavin
Michael Kuhn
Michael Roess
Michelle Perkins
Miguel Head
Mike Turner
Mildred Nicotera

Miles Smith-Morris
Misa Sekiguchi
Moira Garland
Moira Sweeney
Molly Foster
Mona Arshi
Moray Teale
Morayma Jimenez
Moremi Apata-
  Omisore
Moriah Haefner
Morven Dooner
Muireann Maguire
Myles Nolan
N Tsolak
Nan Craig
Nancy Foley
Nancy Jacobson
Nancy Oakes
Nancy Peters
Nancy Sosnow
Nanda Griffioen
Naomi Morauf
Naomi Sparks
Natalia Reyes
Natalie Ricks
Nathalie Adams
Nathalie Atkinson
Nathalie Karagiannis
Nathalie Teitler
Nathan McNamara
Nathan Rowley
Nathan Weida
Neferti Tadiar
Nguyen Phan
Nicholas Brown
Nicholas Jowett
Nicholas Rutherford
Nicholas Smith
Nick James
Nick Nelson &
  Rachel Eley
Nick Sidwell
Nick Twemlow
Nicola Cook
Nicola Hart
Nicola Sandiford
Nicola Scott
Nicole Joy
Nicole Matteini
Nicoletta Asciuto
Nigel Fishburn
Niki Sammut
Nina de la Mer
Nina Nickerson
Nina Todorova
Nudrat Siddiqui
Odilia Corneth
Ohan Hominis
Olivia Scott

Olivia Turon
Pamela Tao
Pat Winslow
Patricia Aronsson
Patrick Hawley
Patrick Hoare
Patrick McGuinness
Paul Cray
Paul Jones
Paul Munday
Paul Nightingale
Paul Robinson
Paul Scott
Paul Thompson and
  Gordon McArthur
Paula McGrath
Pauline Drury
Pavlos Stavropoulos
Penelope Hewett
  Brown
Peter Edwards
Peter Goulborn
Peter Griffin
Peter Halliday
Peter Hudson
Peter McBain
Peter McCambridge
Peter Rowland
Peter Taplin
Peter Wells
Peter Van de Maele
  and Narina Dahms
Petra Stapp
Phil Bartlett
Philip Herbert
Philip Warren
Philip Williams
Philipp Jarke
Phillipa Clements
Phoebe McKenzie
Phoebe Millerwhite
Phyllis Reeve
Pia Figge
Piet Van Bockstal
Prakash Nayak
Rachael de Moravia
Rachael Williams
Rachel Gregory
Rachel Matheson
Rachel Meacock
Rachel Van Riel
Ralph Cowling
Ramona Pulsford
Raymond Manzo
Rebecca Braun
Rebecca Ketcherside
Rebecca Moss
Rebecca O'Reilly
Rebecca Peer
Rebecca Roadman

Rebecca Rosenthal
Rebecca Servadio
Rebecca Shaak
Rebekka Bremmer
Renee Thomas
Rhiannon Armstrong
Rich Sutherland
Richard Clark
Richard Ellis
Richard Gwyn
Richard Mansell
Richard Padwick
Richard Priest
Richard Shea
Richard Soundy
Richard Stubbings
Rick Tucker
Riley & Alyssa
  Manning
Rishi Dastidar
Rita Kaar
Rita O'Brien
Rob Kidd
Robert Gillett
Robert Hannah
Robert Arnott
Roberto Hull
Robin McLean
Robin Taylor
Rogelio Pardo
Roger Newton
Roger Ramsden
Rory Williamson
Rosalind May
Rosalind Ramsay
Rosanna Foster
Rose Pearce
Ross Beaton
Ross MacIntyre
Rowan Bowman
Roxanne O'Del
  Ablett
Roz Simpson
Ruby Thiagarajan
Rupert Ziziros
Ruth Deyermond
Ruth Field
Ryan Day
S Italiano
Sabine Griffiths
Sabine Little
Sally Arkinstall
Sally Baker
Sally Bramley
Sally Ellis
Sally Hemsley
Sally Warner
Sam Gordon
Sam Reese
Sam Southwood

Samuel Crosby
Samuel Wright
Sara Bea
Sara Kittleson
Sara Sherwood
Sara Warshawski
Sarah Arboleda
Sarah Blunden
Sarah Brewer
Sarah Duguid
Sarah Farley
Sarah Lucas
Sarah Manvel
Sarah Pybus
Sarah Spitz
Sarah Stevns
Sasha Dugdale
Scott Astrada
Scott Chiddister
Scott Henkle
Scott Simpson
Sean Kottke
Sez Kiss
Shane Horgan
Shannon Knapp
Sharon Dogar
Shauna Gilligan
Shauna Rogers
Sheila Duffy
Sienna Kang
Simon Pitney
Simon Robertson
Simone Martelossi
SK Grout
Sophie Church

ST Dabbagh
Stacy Rodgers
Stefanie Schrank
Stefano Mula
Stephan Eggum
Stephanie Lacava
Stephanie Miller
Stephanie Smee
Stephen Pearsall
Steve Clough
Steve Dearden
Steve James
Steve Tuffnell
Steven Norton
Steven Vass
Steven Williams
Stewart Eastham
Stuart Phillips
Stuart Wilkinson
Su Bonfanti
Susan Bamford
Susan Clegg
Susan Ferguson
Susan Jaken
Susan Winter
Suzanne Colangelo
 Lillis
Suzanne Kirkham
Sydney Hutchinson
Tamara Larsen
Tania Hershman
Tara Roman
Tasmin Maitland
Teresa Werner
Teri Hoskin

Tess Cohen
Tess McAlister
The Mighty Douche
 Softball Team
Thom Cuell
Thom Keep
Thomas Campbell
Thomas Fritz
Thomas Mitchell
Thomas Phipps
Thomas Smith
Thomas van den Bout
Tian Zheng
Tiffany Lehr
Tim Kelly
Tim Schneider
Tim Scott
Timothy Cummins
Tina Rotherham-
 Winqvist
Toby Halsey
Toby Ryan
Tom Darby
Tom Doyle
Tom Franklin
Tom Gray
Tom Stafford
Tom Whatmore
Tory Jeffay
Tracy Shapley
Trevor Wald
Tricia Durdey
Tricia Pillay
Ursula Dawson
Val & Tom Flechtner

Vanessa Baird
Vanessa Dodd
Vanessa Fernandez
 Greene
Vanessa Fuller
Vanessa Heggie
Vanessa Nolan
Vanessa Rush
Victor Meadowcroft
Victoria Eld
Victoria Goodbody
Victoria Larroque
Vijay Pattisapu
Wendy Langridge
Will Stolton
William Black
William
 Brockenborough
William Dennehy
William Franklin
William Mackenzie
William Richard
William Schwaber
William Sitters
William Wood
Yoora Yi Tenen
Zachary Hope
Zachary Maricondia
Zachary Whyte
Zara Rahman
Zareena Amiruddin
Zoe Taylor
Zoë Brasier

CURRENT & UPCOMING BOOKS